Paul Revere

Boston Patriot

Paul Revere

Boston Patriot

Illustrated by Frank Nicholas

Paul Revere

Boston Patriot

By Augusta Stevenson

Aladdin Paperbacks

First Aladdin Paperbacks edition 1986
Copyright © 1946 by the Bobbs-Merrill Co., Inc.

ALADDIN PAPERBACKS
An imprint of Simon & Schuster Children's Publishing Division
1230 Avenue of the Americas, New York, NY 10020

Manufactured in the United States of America
24 26 28 30 29 27 25 23

Library of Congress Cataloging-in-Publication Data

Stevenson, Augusta
  Paul Rever, Boston patriot.

  Reprint of the ed.: Indianapolis : Bobbs-Merrill.
1984.
  Published 1946 under title: Paul Revere, boy of old
Boston.
  Summary: Presents the boyhood of the well-known Boston
silversmith and patriot of the Revolution, famous for his
ride to warn the countryside of the approaching British.
  1. Revere, Paul, 1735–1818—Childhood and youth—
Juvenile literature. 2. Statesmen—Massachusetts—
Biography—Juvenile literature. 3. Massachusetts—
Biography—Juvenile literature. [1. Revere, Paul,
1735–1818. 2. United States—History—Revolution,
1735–1783—Biography] I. Nicholas, Frank, ill.
II. Title
F69.R43S73 1986   973.3'311'0924 [B] [92] 86-10743

ISBN-13: 978-0-02-042090-3 (pbk.)
ISBN-10: 0-02-042090-0 (pbk.)

To
Ben H. Riker,
Booklover

Illustrations

Full Pages

Numerous smaller illustrations

Contents

CHILDHOOD OF FAMOUS AMERICANS

★ ★ ★

Books by Augusta Stevenson

Paul Revere

Boston Patriot

The Silver Teapot

IT WAS ALMOST seven o'clock in the morning and it was time for the Boston children to start to school in 1744.

It was past time for one nine-year-old boy because he lived away down on the water front.

But this boy, Paul Revere, couldn't find his speller and he was good and worried. He knew what would happen to him if he should go to school without it.

He'd get a whipping for that and he'd get another for being late. Schoolmaster Hicks whipped for almost everything.

"It's your own fault, Paul," said his mother.

"I told you to put your speller on the mantelshelf every night."

"I'll find it," said his sister Debbie.

The family called her Debbie but her name was Deborah. She was named for her mother.

Paul was named for his father, but there was no nickname for him.

Debbie was twelve now, just three years older than Paul. She was fair like her mother.

Paul was dark like his father. He had the same dark-brown hair, and sparkling eyes that were almost black.

Both children were smart and quick. Debbie could usually find everything that was lost, but she had no luck this time.

Then Mrs. Revere helped them. She lighted a candle and peered into dark corners and under chairs and stools.

It was strange they couldn't find the book for there weren't many places to look.

There was only one big room on the first floor. It was the kitchen, dining room and living room, all in one. A storeroom was back of it and bedrooms above. A small hall led to the front door.

Paul was searching now in the hall at one side. No book.

He looked on the stairway that led to the bedrooms on the second floor. No book.

He looked in his bedroom—in his bed and under it. He even looked under the bed where his two younger brothers were still asleep.

There was no speller anywhere, either upstairs or downstairs.

"Tell Master Hicks you'll bring your speller this afternoon," said his mother. "Debbie and I will look for it again."

"He'll whip me anyway."

"He whips too much. I've heard many mothers talk about it."

"He whips hard, too."

Mrs. Revere looked at her handsome dark-haired, dark-eyed boy and sighed.

"You'll have to go, Paul. There's no way out of it."

BUT THERE WAS A WAY OUT

Paul had his hat in his hand and was about to open the door when his father came in from his silversmith shop next door.

Mr. Revere wore a leather apron and a leather cap. He carried a large silver teapot.

"Wait a minute, Paul," he said. "I may need you to deliver this teapot to Mrs. Tarbox."

"Oh, it's beautiful, Father!" cried Debbie.

Mrs. Revere took the teapot in her hands and looked at it closely. "That's a lovely engraving, Paul. It's the old elm tree, the one in the park, isn't it?"

Mr. Revere nodded. "I hope Mrs. Tarbox will

be pleased. She wants it this morning, but I can't leave the shop. I thought Paul might take it to her."

"I will!" cried Paul. "I know where she lives. It's a big white house in a big yard at the end of Anne Street."

"I hate to keep you out of school."

"Oh, that's all right. I can make up my lessons, Father."

"Then you may go. I'll explain your absence to Master Hicks," his father replied. "I am sure he will not mind."

Mr. Revere didn't know he had come just in the nick of time for Paul.

"Do you think it's safe for Paul to carry this silver?" his wife asked. "There are so many thieves in Boston now."

"They live in those old houses in alleys," said Debbie. "And they run out and snatch things from people in broad daylight."

"It's bad," said Mr. Revere, "but they are mostly poor people who can't find work. Many of them steal to get food to eat."

"I won't go through alleys," declared Paul. "I'll go by Anne Street all the way, Father."

"Yes, you must do that. It's farther but there are nice homes all along. He'll have no trouble, Deborah."

"Very well then, I'll pack the teapot," she said.

She wrapped it with a woolen cloth. Then she put it in a basket and covered it with several ears of new corn.

"They'll think I'm a peddler," said Paul. "I should carry a bell and ring it as I go along."

"You don't need a bell," teased Debbie. "Your voice can be heard by vessels at sea."

Paul started to laugh. "I'd do for a foghorn, wouldn't I?"

"Paul," interrupted his father, "give the corn to Mrs. Tarbox. Tell her it's from our garden."

16

Then he hurried back to his shop, and Paul hurried to the door with his basket.

"Paul!" called his mother. "Don't talk to strange sailors!"

Paul knew that strange sailors sometimes stole boys and took them away on ships.

"I'll run if I see one coming."

"And watch for strange peddlers. Some of them are tricky."

"I'll run from them, too, Mother. Good-by! Good-by, Debbie!"

A SAILOR STOPPED HIM

The Revere house was on Fish Street. It faced Clark's Wharf on Boston Harbor.

It was a splendid place for a silversmith. Sea captains were good customers. Rich travelers were good customers also.

They brought bags of silver coins from foreign lands. Mr. Revere melted the coins in his furnace. From the silver sheets he made candlesticks, dishes, buckles, and many other things.

So Mr. Revere was doing very well. There wasn't a better place in Boston for him.

There wasn't a better place for Paul, either. He watched the sailing ships that tied up at Clark's Wharf. He knew where they were from and where they were going. In fact he knew almost everything that went on there.

He stopped at the wharf. There were no strange ships with strange sailors this morning.

Only fishermen were about and no one was afraid of them. These men lived in Boston and folks knew them.

Everything was all right. So Paul walked on, happy and unafraid.

Suddenly, out of a side street came a sailor he had never seen before. Paul didn't have a chance to run. The man stopped in front of him.

18

The sailor smiled broadly. He seemed to be very happy about something.

Paul was afraid the sailor would grab him and take him off to some ship. The boy was so frightened he was trembling.

Then he had a big surprise. The man wasn't even looking at him, but gazing at the corn.

"Roasting ears!" the sailor cried. "They are the first I've seen this year. What will you take for the basket?"

"The—the—basket?"

"Yes, indeed! I want 'em all. I'm so hungry for corn my mouth waters."

"I—I—it's for a lady."

"I'll pay twice as much."

"My folks——"

"Oh, bother your folks! I want that corn and I'm going to have it."

As he reached for it, Paul turned and ran back the way he had come.

The sailor ran after him, but when he came to the corner Paul had disappeared.

THEN A PEDDLER STOPPED HIM

Paul had run through an empty warehouse, out the back door and into an alley.

This alley was so narrow that he could almost touch the houses on each side as he ran along.

They were all old. They seemed nearly ready to fall down. Some had no doors. Broken windows were stuffed with dirty rags.

There was no one about, but Paul was frightened. He imagined eyes were watching him.

People said these houses were full of thieves. What if one should suddenly reach out and grab his basket of corn?

And what if the sailor found him!

There was plenty to worry a nine-year-old boy with a valuable piece of silver.

Then the very thing he feared happened. An arm was thrust out from a doorway and a strong hand held him fast.

A rough-looking man followed the arm and hand. He was a peddler with a basket of salted codfish and a small bell.

He dropped Paul's arm and smiled.

"You needn't be scared of me, lad. I won't do you no harm. I saw your corn and I says to myself we might make a bargain."

"I don't understand——"

"Well now, here's the plain truth. You don't know how to peddle. Where's your bell?"

"I've got a loud voice——"

"No good; folks is used to bells. So I jest sells your corn for you. It's early for roasting ears. I can get a good price. Then I'll give you what's over the price you're asking. I mean I'll divide it with you. Ain't that fair enough?"

"I promised my father——"

"Tut, tut! Don't give that a thought. Your father didn't know you would meet me. And I'm the man who can sell anything for twice the price. Here, let me have a look at those ears."

Paul knew he had to do something quickly. In another minute the peddler would find the tea-pot hidden under the corn.

Then he used every bit of that sea-going voice of his and yelled for help.

Almost at once the alley was full of strange-looking men and women. They came running from the old houses like bees from a hive.

"Who screamed?" they asked one another.

But no one knew what had happened. Paul had fled and the peddler had disappeared.

WOMEN WORSE THAN CORN

Paul had good luck at last. When he escaped from the alley he found he was on Anne Street.

"I won't have any trouble here," he thought. "Nice houses and nice women like my mother, coming and going with market baskets."

Paul was wrong. He had plenty of trouble here, with these nice women, too.

They were determined to buy his corn. They wouldn't take "No" for an answer. They teased him for just two ears or even just one.

They took corn out of his basket to examine it. They pulled off the husks.

It was too much for Paul—he ran. And he didn't stop until he came to the Tarbox yard.

Mrs. Tarbox was delighted with the teapot. She liked the shape and the engraving of the old elm tree his father had put on it.

She was pleased also to have the new corn.

"Please tell your folks it was very kind of them to send me corn from your garden."

"It was to hide the silver. Mother was afraid I would have trouble."

24

"You didn't, did you?"

"Oh, no. I just came along. I didn't have any trouble to speak of."

At noon during lunch Paul told his family about his adventures.

When he came to the last part, what he had said to Mrs. Tarbox, his father roared with laughter. "No trouble! Ha, ha, ha!"

"Nothing to speak of!" repeated his mother. "Ha, ha, ha!"

She laughed so hard she forgot to say she had found the speller in the garden.

Mr. Revere now put his hand on Paul's head lovingly. "I'm sorry, son. It was all my fault. I should have listened to your mother."

"He'll carry no more silver so far from home," declared Deborah. "At least, not until he is a little older."

A Strict
Schoolmaster

YOU DIDN'T CATCH any Boston boys staying in
school after it was out at 5:00 P.M.

Paul and his friend Mickey Weems were off
for the wharves by 5:02 P.M. daily.

But this afternoon, here was Paul still waiting, and it was all of 5:15.

The master had kept Michael Weems in, and
Paul wouldn't think of going without him.

Ten more minutes passed. Paul began to
worry. A whaling ship was to sail at six o'clock
sharp. The boys didn't want to miss that.

This was the last whaler that would sail this
year. They just couldn't miss it.

"Mr. Hicks hadn't any right to keep Mickey so late. He hadn't done anything wrong," Paul thought angrily.

"Mickey's copybook didn't suit Mr. Hicks. But good gracious, he'd whip you if you forgot to dot an *i* or cross a *t*!"

The two boys were the same age, ten years. Both loved the water and there was plenty of that around Boston. There was almost nothing else. The woods was far away.

In the summer the two boys swam, dived, rowed, and fished.

In the winter they often skated and played ice shinny together.

They watched the fishing boats go out in the early morning.

They watched freighters load and unload.

They watched the large fast ships sail away to England with passengers.

They saw sloops, brigs, and schooners leaving

for New York City and Philadelphia, loaded with freight and passengers, too.

But the most exciting of all was the sailing of a whaler. There was always a large crowd on the wharf to see the whaling men leave.

They were starting on a dangerous journey. They would be in frozen seas and among icebergs that could crush their ship.

It was also dangerous work. A whale fisherman never knew whether he would kill the whale or the whale would kill him.

Of course Mickey and Paul wanted to wave at these brave men as they sailed away.

"Well, I guess we don't wave this year," Paul said to himself at 5:30.

Five more minutes, then Mickey came. He was a tall, good-looking boy with light hair and plenty of freckles. He had a good-natured smile and his blue eyes squinted a little.

Paul didn't waste any time on questions.

"Come along, Mickey!" he said. "We'll miss the whaler."

"I was afraid of that."

"Did Mr. Hicks whip you?" asked Paul as they hurried down to the wharf.

"No, but he will if I don't make better lines in my copybook. He said he'd give me one more week to improve."

"It's all in the way you hold your lead. Look."

He took a piece of sharpened lead from his pocket and showed Mickey how to hold it.

"Father showed me. He holds it this way when he rules lines."

"I've tried that way but my lines still run downhill. Look at my book, Paul."

"Your lines aren't straight, that's a fact. They are too heavy, too."

"Mr. Hicks scolded me for that. Mother used to say my eyesight was bad."

"Why, of course! I didn't think of that. You

29

have to squint to see anything. Why don't you tell the master?"

"He wouldn't believe me. He'd whip me for making excuses."

"Then I'll make a new book for you and rule it," Paul offered.

Mickey shook his head. "He would know I didn't rule it. He'd whip me for cheating."

"It isn't cheating, on account of your eyes. Anyone would tell you that."

"Well, maybe not. I hadn't thought of it that way," Mickey replied doubtfully.

The boys had now reached the wharf. Many people were standing around on the wharf. They had come to see the whaler, too.

"Look at the crowd!" cried Paul. "I guess everyone in Boston came down. The whaler is about ready to sail, too."

"Let's crowd in and wave to the fishermen," cried Mickey excitedly.

One week from that day Zachariah Hicks called for the writing books. One by one, frightened boys took them up to his desk and stood there trembling.

"Jonathan Mayberry," Mr. Hicks called sharply, "your writing is fair but your lines are much too heavy."

"Yes, sir."

"I've told you about this again and again. Now a hickory switch will teach you. You will stay in tonight."

"Yes, sir."

"Ebenezer Tuttle, you refuse to cross your small *t's*, don't you?"

"Oh! I guess I forgot."

"A hickory switch may cause you to remember, too. Stay in."

"Yes, sir."

"Paul Revere, your letters are carefully made.

31

Your lines are straight and thin. They are an equal distance apart."

He looked at Paul now with suspicion.

"Did your father rule it?"

"No, sir," Paul replied.

"It's lucky for you he didn't."

"Yes, sir."

"Michael Weems, this new book doesn't look like your last one. Did you rule these lines?"

"I—I practiced at home."

"I didn't ask you that. I asked if you ruled this book. Well, did you?"

"No, sir."

"Who ruled it?"

Mickey didn't answer. The schoolmaster turned to Paul.

"Did you rule it?"

"Yes, sir."

"So, you two thought you'd deceive me, did you?" he demanded.

"I didn't write a single word," said Paul. "I didn't think it was wrong to make lines."

"You'll change your mind this afternoon. A hickory stick will help you. Stay in, both of you."

Paul and Mickey were now alone with the schoolmaster. The other boys had been whipped and sent home.

Zachariah was selecting a fresh switch from the bundle in the corner.

The boys hoped and hoped that something would happen: a cyclone or anything to distract the master's attention.

But the cyclone didn't come, and Mr. Hicks told them to take off their coats. Then he lifted his stick and beckoned to Mickey.

"Wait a minute, Master!" cried Paul. He had thought of something at last. It wasn't a cyclone, but maybe it would stop him.

"I have something to tell you," he hurried on. "I almost forgot it. The preachers are coming tomorrow morning."

"What is this? You say the preachers are coming here—to this school?"

34

"Yes, sir, all of them, at eight o'clock, to visit."

"Who told you?"

"The pastor of Christ Church. My father sent me there last night with a silver candlestick. Mr. Cutler said they would examine our copybooks."

"Is that the reason you ruled Mickey's?"

"No, sir. It was on account of his eyes. He can't see to make straight lines. I heard his mother say that."

"Why didn't you tell me that, Mickey?"

The boys were astonished. The master's voice was actually kind.

"I—I guess I was afraid."

Master Hicks put down his switch.

"You boys may go now. I shall have much to do for tomorrow."

"Well, for goodness sake!" exclaimed Paul when the door was closed behind them.

"Yes, indeed! For goodness sake!" echoed the amazed Mickey.

35

The ministers had come. They sat on the platform looking very grand and solemn.

They wore black robes and queer-shaped black hats. Each of them also wore a long, white, curled wig.

Frightened young boys had to spell and read for the ministers.

Nervous older boys had to work arithmetic problems for them.

After this the ministers examined the copybooks, carefully and slowly.

Finally Mr. Cutler called Paul Revere and Michael Weems to the platform.

He said their writing was the best in the school, and their lines the best in Boston.

"We have visited other schools," he went on, "and not one could show us writing books ruled so straight and true.

"Therefore, we have decided to give you the

prizes. The Reverend Jonathan Mayhew will now present them."

He turned to Mr. Mayhew but that gentleman was whispering with Master Hicks.

Then an amazing thing happened. Mickey began to speak.

"I can't take a prize, Mr. Cutler. I didn't make the lines in my book. A—a friend—ruled them."

"Oh!" exclaimed the astonished preacher. "Oh, Ah, indeed!"

"I ruled his book, sir," said Paul. "I can't take a prize either."

The Reverend Mr. Mayhew now came forward. There was a smile on his face and his voice was kind.

"Boys, your master has explained this matter. Michael, because of your poor eyesight we will judge your book by your writing only. Your writing is excellent. So I now present this medal to you."

"Thank you, sir."

"Paul, I now present this medal to you."

"Thank you, sir."

On each shining brass medal was engraved a strong and mighty tree.

Mr. Mayhew said it was the "Tree of Knowledge." But the two boys agreed it was really the old elm, the one in the Boston Common.

Climbing the Rigging

ONE BY ONE some half-dozen fishermen went into the wharfmaster's cabin on Hitchbourn Wharf.

They entered quietly so no one would notice them. It was a secret meeting. No Tory must know about it. They talked quietly so no one outside could hear.

These men had been having a hard time because they were patriots and didn't want a king.

The Tories wouldn't buy their fish because every Tory wanted a king.

The royal government sent patriots to jail for the least thing. Sometimes just because a Tory accused them.

Now the fishermen—about their taxes. The king has made a new law which would raise them. It was called the 'New Fish Law.'

"The law puts a tax on every fish we catch," fishermen complained. "It also taxes our hooks and nets and boats."

"We can't make enough to live on," they said. "Our children will go hungry."

They have talked about it for weeks. Now they were meeting to see what could be done about the New Fish Law.

Some thought that they should refuse to pay the tax, and Mr. Fogarty, the wharfmaster, agreed with them completely.

But others thought this would be dangerous. "The government would arrest every man who refused," they declared.

"Let him arrest us!" cried Mr. Fogarty boldly. "The jails will soon be so full he'll have no place to put us."

40

"Aye!" cried one. "He'll be frightened for his own safety when he sees so many against him."

While they were talking about this, two boys swam to the wharf and climbed to the dock.

They had left their clothes back of Mr. Fogarty's cabin, so they came here to dress.

They heard voices inside but paid no attention at first. Presently, however, they heard things that astonished them.

"I have no respect for this king," said a voice. "He's a stupid dunce."

"He's worse, he's a knave," said another voice. "He'd take our last cent and put it in his own pocket."

"Aye! Aye!" cried others.

"I have a plan," said the wharfmaster, "but I can't tell you now. It would take too long. Come to my house tonight."

The men agreed to meet at seven. Then they left the cabin one by one.

"My father can't pay his taxes," said Mickey. "He doesn't know what to do."

"My father can't pay his either, and he's worried," said Paul.

They were silent for a moment, then Paul burst out. "Mickey, I haven't got a bit of use for that king over in England!"

"Hush, Paul! You mustn't say that. You'll get into trouble. He's our king. He owns this country you know."

"The fishermen talked against him."

"They won't talk that way when there's a Tory around. But you will, Paul, you're such a hot-headed patriot."

"I know I am. But I know something else too: I'll never repeat a word of what the fishermen said in the cabin."

"I never will, either," Mickey promised. "Here's my hand on it."

"Here's mine."

The boys had finished dressing and were about to leave when two seamen passed by.

"Look!" whispered Paul. "That's Captain Bootle and his mate."

Mickey nodded. "That means the "Alice" has landed and there's no one aboard."

They were grinning with delight and their eyes were shining with mischief. Each knew exactly what the other was thinking. What a chance to climb the rigging!

The "Alice" was a sloop and didn't have so many ropes as larger vessels. She had just enough ropes to suit the boys.

Then here were Captain Bootle and his mate going ashore. They would spend the day with their families, as they always did.

It was the chance of a lifetime. Of course they knew it was against ship rules. And they knew they'd be punished if they were caught.

Their mother had told them how dangerous it was and how some boys had fallen and had been hurt.

Their fathers had punished them once before for going aboard ship. Mr. Fogarty threatened to call the constable if they ever tried to climb the rigging again.

It was all forgotten now. In another two minutes they had reached the "Alice" and were about to go aboard.

But just then a sailor appeared on the deck. The boys hid quickly out of sight behind an old skiff at the wharf.

This sailor was the ugliest man they had ever seen. He was very tall and very thin. He had bright red hair and a large wart on his big nose.

His mouth spread from ear to ear, almost, and his lips were thick.

His ears were so long both boys noticed them. And if he didn't wear large hoop earrings!

44

This strange-looking man acted strangely, too. He looked about by jerking his head this way and that.

Then he thrust his hand quickly into the front of his blouse and took out a red moneybag.

It was full. The boys could see it was bulging with coins though they had only one look.

Then he thrust the bag into his breeches pocket so quickly they hardly saw him do it.

He looked about again, stretching his long neck and jerking his head this way and that.

He looked at his big pistol and put it back in his belt. Then he jumped to the wharf and hurried to the street.

"I guess he's afraid someone will know he has money," said Mickey.

Now they went aboard the little vessel and started to climb the rigging. Up, up, up, clear up to the crosspiece on the tall mast.

This was fun! It was thrilling to be up high in

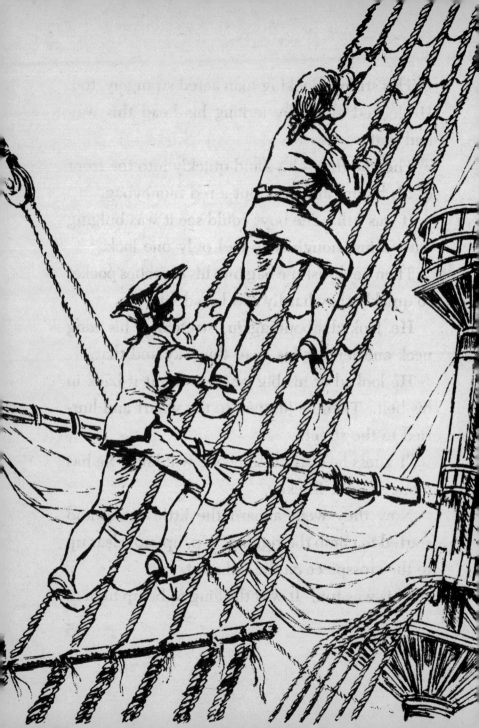

the blue sky. It was thrilling to see the blue water so far below.

The boys wanted to shout and laugh and sing, but they didn't dare. They were afraid that Mr. Fogarty might hear them.

They were swinging on ropes when they heard loud shouting from the deck below.

"Come down! Come out of the rigging!" yelled Captain Bootle.

"Come down or I'll get the constable!" yelled the wharfmaster.

The boys came down as fast as they could. When they reached the deck they faced two angry men.

"You know better than to climb the rigging, Paul Revere!" cried Mr. Fogarty. "You know better, too, Mickey Weems! I've told you and told you to keep off, but the minute my back is turned up you go."

"If one of you had been hurt, I would be punished. They'd put me in prison for the rest of my life," said Captain Bootle.

The boys said they knew they wouldn't fall. They knew how to climb rigging.

Mr. Fogarty shook a finger at Paul. He was very angry. "How do you happen to be so smart, Paul Revere? Your own cousin fell from rigging and broke his neck. That was when your granddaddy owned this wharf and he had told the boys to keep out of rigging.

"Captain Bootle, these boys ought to be punished. Their fathers ought to know."

"They shall know, I'll tell them myself to make certain. I want to see Mr. Revere anyway about some coins. You boys wait here till I get my bag."

He went into his cabin. Mr. Fogarty shook a finger at them again. "And don't you move from that spot, either one of you," he ordered.

They didn't.

It was at least fifteen minutes before Captain Bootle came back.

"I've been looking for my coin bag," he explained hastily. "I couldn't find it—it's been stolen!"

"I didn't notice anyone on your sloop," said Mr. Fogarty.

"We did!" cried Mickey. "A sailor!"

"Was it a red bag?" asked Paul.

"It was. Red cloth."

The boys told what they had seen. When they came to the red hair and wart-on-his-nose and rings-in-his-ears, the Captain stopped them.

"That's enough. I know him. He used to be in my crew. Which way did he go when he left the wharf, boys?"

The boys hadn't watched. But Paul was sure the sailor would go to a silversmith shop first.

"He'll want the coins melted so you can't

claim them, Captain. He would say they were his and no one could tell from a sheet of silver."

"I think you are right, but there are several silversmiths in Boston."

"We know them all," said Paul.

"We'll find him," said Mickey.

"If you do I'll give each of you a good reward. I'm going after the constable. Meet me here on this wharf as soon as you find the thief."

The boys went running. In no time at all they were peeping through a window in Mr. Revere's silversmith shop.

There stood the sailor! The red bag was in his hand. It was still bulging with coins.

Mr. Revere was back of the counter. Paul could tell at once that his father wasn't pleased with his customer.

"But I tell you I can't melt them this minute," Mr. Revere was saying. "I already have something in my furnace."

50

The boys didn't wait to hear more. They went running back to the wharf.

So they didn't hear the sailor tell Mr. Revere that he would pay him extra if he would melt his coins at once.

Again the smith refused the sailor's urgent request. He said the delay would disappoint a good customer.

"But my ship is leaving soon, in an hour or so!" the sailor exclaimed.

"I'll have your silver melted and ready for you when you return on your next voyage. I will make it up, too. Have you decided what you want made, a silver mug perhaps?"

The sailor didn't want anything made, he said. All he wanted was the melted silver and he wanted that quickly. He threw his bag on the counter angrily.

"I'm sorry, but that's the best I can do for you, sir," Mr. Revere declared.

The sailor drew his pistol and aimed it directly at Mr. Revere.

"Take that stuff out of the furnace and put mine in!" he ordered angrily.

At that moment the door opened and the constable entered with Captain Bootle. Both carried pistols in their hands.

Quick as a cat, the sailor jumped over the counter. He ran through the shop and out the back door into an alley.

The others followed but the thief had disappeared. The constable searched for him but in vain. There wasn't a trace of the thief.

"It's easy to disappear in Boston," the constable said. "There are so many crooked streets and alleys."

It was dark before they gave up the hunt. Then Captain Bootle came back to the shop and Mr. Revere gave him the red bag.

"These boys have earned their reward, Mr.

Revere. But there's another matter that must be settled first. I found them up in my ship's rigging this morning."

"Paul," said his father sharply, "you cannot go on any wharf for one month."

"Yes, sir."

"Mickey, I shall ask your father to punish you in the same way."

"Yes, sir."

Captain Bootle took a handful of coins from the bag and offered them to the boys.

"We don't want money, Captain," said Paul. "You bring in ponies sometimes, so if you don't mind, we'd like to have one."

"One! How can that be? There are two of you," the captain replied.

"We hated to ask for two," said Mickey. "We will take turns riding."

"You shall each have one. I'll bring them on my next trip."

"Oh! Oh!" cried the delighted boys. "Thank you, Captain! Thank you!"

"But keep out of my rigging."

"Yes, Captain, we will."

They kept their word. Mr. Fogarty had no more trouble with them, either before the ponies came or afterward.

Two Young Apprentices

Mrs. Revere had gone to visit her cousin, Miss Martha Hitchbourn, out on the Lexington Road. So Debbie was keeping house.

She was a pretty girl of seventeen now, with golden hair and blue eyes. She was a good cook and could use the long-handled skillet almost as well as her mother. Debbie always kept her dress out of the fire, too.

But she wasn't so smart with her baking. She'd think about something else and forget the salt or sugar or soda.

Mrs. Revere spoke of this matter the day she left. "Keep your mind on your work, Debbie," she cautioned. "Don't try to plan a picnic while you are getting a meal.

"Remember to have meals on time. Your father and Paul are busy. They can't be kept waiting."

Debbie remembered this when she started supper. But when she was making corn bread she remembered something else and laughed.

"What are you laughing at?" asked her sister Frances, who was thirteen.

"Oh, I thought of the corn bread Mother took with her to Martha's—a whole skilletful to eat on Sunday. She took butter and honey, too. She said she'd starve if she didn't."

"Wouldn't it be a joke if Martha walked into her room while she was eating?"

Both laughed heartily at this. And it was funny because their cousin owned a large farm and had plenty to eat except on Sunday.

"Doesn't Martha get hungry on Sunday, Debbie?" Frances asked.

"Of course she does, but she is a Puritan, you know. They don't think anyone should eat much on the Lord's Day. And they think it's wrong to laugh and joke on Sunday, too."

"Father laughs and jokes on Sunday."

"Father isn't really a Puritan. You see, he came from France and they don't have that church over there. And now Mother isn't much of a Puritan herself."

"She jokes and laughs on Sunday."

"She'd better not at Martha's."

Both laughed again. It was very funny to think of anyone bossing Mother, but then Martha was older, five years older.

Suddenly Debbie remembered she hadn't put salt in her bread. "I thought of it just in time! We're going to have company for supper, too. Mickey is coming home with Paul."

"Goody! I like to have him come. He tells funny stories," said Frances.

"Father asked him this morning before they started to the woods."

"I hope they shoot a lot of game. I just love fried rabbit. And wouldn't it be wonderful if they shot a deer?"

"I don't know how they'd carry it. Their ponies could hardly carry them."

Both girls laughed as they remembered how Paul looked on Bootle, with his feet almost touching the ground.

And how Mickey looked on Captain, with his feet fairly dragging.

They were still giggling when their father came in to ask if the boys had come.

Mr. Revere said he couldn't wait. He would have to eat now because a customer was coming a little later.

He rested till the corn bread was ready and talked to his daughters.

He said he had been very busy, but he was glad

Paul took the day off. Paul had been working hard ever since he came into the shop.

"That was over a year ago," said Debbie, "when he was just thirteen."

"He's the best apprentice I ever had. I believe he'll make a fine silversmith. He'll be an artist."

"I'm an artist, too," said Debbie. "No one can beat me with a long-handled skillet."

She laughed but her father answered gravely, "You are indeed, Debbie. It's very pretty the way you manage it. I believe I'll make an engraving of you holding your long-handled skillet on some silver piece."

Now the bread was done. So the younger children were called and presently the family sat down to eat supper.

But Debbie was disappointed because Paul and Mickey liked her hot skillet-fried bread. They always bragged about it but now they weren't here to enjoy it.

Supper had been over an hour. Mr. Revere had seen his customer and was back. Then Paul came, but he was alone.

He said Mickey had to work to make up the time he had lost that day. "He was sorry about supper, Debbie. But he's an apprentice now in a tailor shop. He said his master would be angry if he stopped to eat."

"Won't the tailor give him any supper, Paul?" Frances asked.

"He'll probably get a hunk of old bread and a piece of cheese."

"No master has the right to starve his apprentice," said Mr. Revere. "And this Simon Yardley is said to be well off."

"He is, and he's the meanest man in Boston, too. Mickey told me all about him today. It's terrible the way he treats Mickey.

"He never gives him enough to eat. Mickey

said he was hungry all the time. Mr. Yardley beats him, too."

Mr. Revere jumped to his feet. "I wish I had known this long ago!"

"That isn't all, Father. The tailor shop is dark and the old miser won't light a candle until nighttime. But if a seam isn't straight Mickey gets a beating."

"He can't see very well anyway," said Debbie.

"It's too bad Mickey is bound to that miser," Paul said. "He has to stay three more years. He wouldn't have gone there, but he needed work."

"Yes, he did," said Mr. Revere. "His father was lost at sea and his mother died soon after. Well, I'm going to do something about all this. I'll try to persuade Mr. Yardley to give him up. Then Mickey can live here with us and go into my shop."

"That's splendid, Father! I'll tell Mickey to-morrow night."

62

Young John and Tom thought they had waited long enough to hear about the hunt.

"Did you find a deer?" asked John.

"How many rabbits did you shoot?" asked Tom curiously.

"We didn't get anything, boys. Some Indians drove us out of the forest."

"Indians!" cried the others.

"There was a band of them, some fifteen or twenty. One of the Indians spoke English and he told us to get out. He said the forest belonged only to them."

"I am thankful they didn't harm you boys," said Mr. Revere.

"They took our ponies. We had to walk all the way home."

"You were almost walking when you left," teased Debbie.

"I wanted Captain," said John.

"I wanted Bootle," said Tom.

"We meant to give them to you. We decided we were a little too large for them now."

"A little!" cried Debbie. "Ha, ha!"

"That's enough teasing, Debbie. Get Paul's supper," said her father.

"Oh, I'm sorry, Paul. I forgot."

"Other hunters have had trouble with Indians lately," said Mr. Revere. "The governor fears we will have a war with them within a year."

"If we do I want to go, Father. I'm over fourteen now," said Paul.

"Yes, you are old enough. I won't refuse if you are needed."

"Mickey will join, too," Paul added. "I'll tell him tomorrow night."

TOO LATE

The next night was too late to tell Mickey anything. He had disappeared.

64

The tailor had sent him on an errand early in the morning before daylight. He was to take a coat to Long Wharf, to a sea captain.

He didn't come back. The sea captain didn't get his coat. It was still in the shop.

Paul was heartbroken. What had happened to his friend? Had he run away? Or had he been kidnapped by sailors?

Mr. Revere closed his shop and hunted for Mickey himself. He talked to sailors, captains and wharfmasters. He asked them to watch every ship that sailed.

They all promised that they would be looking out for a tall thin boy of fourteen, with fair hair and blue eyes that squinted.

The town crier went through the streets ringing his bell and crying out Mickey's name.

"Boy disappears! Name, Michael Weems! Aged fourteen and six months! Tall, thin, light hair, blue eyes, freckles, nice smile, polite!"

Ding, dong, ding dong!

"Tell constable what you know! Tell constable what you hear!"

Ding, dong, ding dong!

A month passed and there was no news. No one had been to the constable. No sailor had seen Mickey. No captain had heard of him. No wharfmaster thought he had gone to sea.

Then Paul gave up. There was no use—Mickey wouldn't come back.

He often shed tears when he was alone and Debbie shed tears when she was alone.

Frances didn't wait to be alone. She cried whenever they talked about him.

Mr. and Mrs. Revere prayed the Lord to watch over Mickey and keep him from harm.

Boy Bell
Ringers

IT WAS EARLY evening in July, but it was still light when Paul started to Christ Church (often called the Old North).

He had been one of their bell ringers for the past year, ever since he was fourteen.

Mr. Murset was the chimesmaster and had taught Paul and the other boy ringers.

He was still teaching them, for that matter. There was no end to the things they had to learn. To ring chimes with ropes wasn't easy.

There were eight large bells and each had a different tone. When the right ropes were pulled at the right time they gave out a sweet chiming.

Everyone said the Old North bells had the sweetest ring of all the bells in the Boston churches.

Paul liked to hear people say that. He was proud of these bells himself. There was one particular bell he liked better than the other seven, much better.

Of course that was the bell he always rang. He smiled as he thought of the arguments he had had over this matter with the other ringers.

Each thought his own bell gave out the clearest and sweetest note.

Paul liked bell ringing. He thought how very much he liked it as he walked along.

How different it would have been had he gone to war! Thank goodness, the governor had made peace with the Indians.

He was sure Mickey would have liked ringing. Poor Mickey! In all this time, a year now, no one had heard of him.

Then he thought of his own special bell again. Would he ever be able to get its best tone? He wondered if Mr. Murset would let him practice more than their regular one night a week. . . .

Tonight was the second time this week. This was to practice for the big funeral tomorrow.

The wealthy shipowner, Mr. Jeramiah Worthington, had died and they would have to toll his age, ninety-five years.

That meant ninety-five pulls of the rope of one bell, and there must be the same interval between each pull. It would be difficult but the boys would take turns tolling.

They would ring the chimes just before the services. He hoped they would be able to do it exactly right. Folks would be listening all over Boston because Mr. Worthington was a very important man.

Paul had now reached the Worthington home,

a mansion in a large yard. There was a flower garden on the east side with walks and benches.

There was a fence around the yard, but one could enter the garden through a high iron gate. It opened on the street and passers-by often stopped to admire it. It was wrought iron with a pattern that looked like lace. Paul thought it was beautiful.

He always stopped to look at it. He wanted to stop now, but he was a little late. He'd have to hurry on.

A TORY BOY INSULTS PAUL

Paul had gone but a few steps when suddenly he turned and went back. He just had to see how that lacework looked in the dim light.

Another minute and he was gazing at it with delight. "It is wonderful. It is delicate and fairy-like," he thought.

71

He hoped that someday, when he was a smith, he could make something as lovely as this.

"What do you want? Why are you prowling around here?" someone suddenly asked.

A boy came out of the shadows in the garden and up to the gate.

He was about Paul's age and he was English. Paul could tell that from his voice.

He was dressed like those two English boys who came on the last fast ship. Paul didn't think much of this style. It wasn't American, so, of course, it didn't suit him.

"This is my grandfather's place," the boy was saying. "People aren't allowed to come in here from the street."

Paul explained why he had stopped. Then he said he was on his way to Christ Church to practice on the bells.

"Oh! I've heard of those bells. I heard of them in England."

He opened the gate now and stood leaning against it.

"So you are one of those boy bell ringers!" he continued haughtily.

Paul didn't like the way the boy said this but he answered politely. He added that his name was Paul Revere.

"My name is Reginald Worthington Ramsey. I came over from London a week ago with my mother. She is terribly upset about the bell ringers for the funeral."

"Oh, she doesn't need to worry. The chimes-master is Mr. Murset and he's the best chimes-master in Boston."

"She says it's too bad we can't have bell ringers from England."

"Mr. Murset studied in England. He has rung all the famous bells over there."

Reginald shook his head. "An American can't ring properly."

"Why not?" Paul was angry now.

"Because most Americans aren't smart. They are really quite stupid."

"Who told you that?"

"It's the talk in London. I've heard it said a hundred times."

"Don't they know that nearly all of our important men were educated in England, in English colleges?"

"Oh, I suppose there are some such men in Boston, but only a few."

"There are a good many and the most of them are patriots, too."

"My grandfather said these American patriots were blockheads."

If the English boy could have seen Paul Revere's angry black eyes, he would have stopped then and there. Paul's broad and powerful shoulders might have been a warning also.

But the boy went right on with his insults.

74

"Why, my grandfather wouldn't buy fish from patriots. He said he'd see them starve first. I don't blame him. I'd let them starve, too. They are nothing but trash."

"Come out from behind that gate!" As he spoke, Paul reached out a strong and powerful hand. He seized Reginald by his coat collar and pulled him outside to the street.

"Now then, you Tory, fight!"

PAUL THROWS A BOMB

In a small room in the back part of Christ Church, the bell ringers waited for Paul.

The oldest one was John Dyer who was nineteen. The others were between that and fifteen.

They were nice-looking and well-behaved youths. Their clothes looked nice also, even though they wore their work suits.

Pulling ropes on a summer night was hot,

sweaty work. But every boy wore a clean full-sleeved white shirt and clean cotton knee breeches.

It was more than just work. It was a lesson in the great art of bell ringing. They thought they were lucky to have a chance to learn.

This evening each boy bragged a little about his own special bell, but not very much.

They talked more about Paul Revere. They wondered why he hadn't come.

"Paul's usually the first one here," said Joseph Snelling.

"I know he's coming," declared Josiah Flagg. "He said he was this morning."

Josiah's brother Barth nodded and said he heard Paul say it.

Mr. Murset came in for the third time and looked about the room. "Paul hasn't come yet, I see. I'm afraid we can't wait much longer."

"He'll have to pay a fine if he's late," said John

Brown. "That's one of the rules of the Bell Ringers' Club."

"It will be a good joke on him," smiled John Dyer. "He proposed the fine himself."

"All right, boys. Let's go up to the rope room now," Mr. Murset commanded. "I'll take Paul's bell myself."

Just then the door opened and Paul came in.

The boys looked at him, astonished. His nose was bloody. His face was bruised and scratched. His once white shirt was now dirty and torn. His breeches were covered with mud. A buckle was missing from one shoe.

"I'm sorry I'm late, Mr. Murset. I was in a fight," he said breathlessly.

The boys were still more astonished. Paul wasn't a fighter.

"Tell us about it, Paul," said Mr. Murset kindly. "Whom did you fight?"

"A Tory!" Paul answered fiercely and his

black eyes flashed with anger. "He said patriots were nothing but trash and blockheads!"

There were angry exclamations from the other boys. They were all red-hot patriots. They surrounded Paul and asked questions.

Mr. Murset saw they were too excited to practice now so he proposed they all sit down and talk things over.

Then Paul told them everything. And when he came to the way Jeramiah Worthington had treated patriot workers, there were more angry exclamations from the boys.

"And he was an American," said John Dyer. "He was born in Boston."

"He was a Tory!" cried Paul. "And I won't ring for his funeral."

It was like throwing a bomb into the room. Only instead of an explosion you could have heard a pin drop.

Everyone was astonished. No one there had

ever heard of anyone refusing to ring the bells for a funeral.

"You musn't say such a thing, Paul," said the chimesmaster.

"I do say it, and I mean to stick to it," Paul replied defiantly.

"But we can't ring the chimes without you!" the other ringers chorused.

"I can't help it—I won't ring. And I hope the others will refuse also."

"Boys," pleaded Mr. Murset, "don't listen to Paul. It would be a terrible thing for this church. The Worthingtons are wealthy people. They might even leave the church."

The boys didn't answer. In fact, they scarcely looked at him or heard him. Their eyes were fixed on Paul Revere.

Now Paul spoke again. "I hereby and now call a meeting of the Bell Ringers' Club. We will meet in the back room, Mr. Murset."

The door leading to the little back room was closed. Only a murmur of boys' voices was heard in the hall.

Mr. Timothy Cutler, the minister, was now with Mr. Murset. Both were worried and showed it plainly.

"How long have they been in there, Mr. Murset?" he asked.

"A good fifteen minutes, sir."

"It's a very bad situation. Mr. Worthington's family asked for the chimes. They want his favorite hymn," Pastor Cutler said.

"I know, but I said everything I could. However, they may listen to you, Mr. Cutler."

"I suppose we could omit the chimes and you could toll the bell yourself. That is, of course, if they refuse. But I don't think they will, they wouldn't dare."

Now the door opened and the boys came out

81

into the hall. One look at their grave young faces and both men feared the worst.

The spokesman for the group was the oldest one, John Dyer. "Mr. Cutler, we have taken a vote. We refuse to ring the bells for Mr. Worthington's funeral."

"But you can't refuse! You are employed by this church to ring when you are needed."

"We can quit," said Paul Revere.

"That wouldn't be fair, Paul. Mr. Murset has trained you. You certainly owe something to him for his help."

"We know that, Mr. Cutler," Paul replied, "and we are all sorry we have to take this stand. But we can't help to honor a man who mistreated patriots," he declared.

"You don't realize what you are doing, boys! You don't realize how very serious this is! What will people say? Why, such a thing has never happened before anywhere. I wish you would talk it over again, boys. Don't you think they should, Mr. Murset?"

"I do indeed, Mr. Cutler. They should take more time."

"It won't do any good," declared John. "Everyone voted against ringing."

"Well then, since I cannot persuade you, we will omit the chimes. And you can toll the bell, Mr. Murset," said the minister.

"Mr. Cutler, I refuse."

"What is this? You refuse?"

"I do. I am a patriot, too. These boys have shown me my duty."

The minister looked at Mr. Murset for a full minute. Then he turned and walked slowly out of the room.

The next day no chimes were rung and no bell was tolled for the funeral of the Tory, Jeramiah Worthington.

From Silver to Iron

THE DAY after the funeral of the rich Tory, things began to happen.

Early in the morning a fine coach stopped in front of the Revere house and the coachman went into the shop.

He stuttered and stammered. "Uh—uh—Mr. Revere, I—I—— Now about that silver jewel box for Mrs. Grand—— Uh—uh—it seems she won't be wanting it now."

"I understand."

The coachman looked about and lowered his voice. "She's angry about the bells, sir. She says your boy put the others up to it."

84

"I think he did."

"Glory be! I'm a patriot myself even if I am working for a Tory. And, Mister, I'm that proud of those bell ringers I could burst. I've been singing to my horses all morning."

"I've been playing a tune with my hammer."

"You've a right to be happy. You have a son to be proud of. Well, good day to you, sir! And may you have good luck in spite of these Tories."

As he went out a young lady came in. She was a maid in another rich Tory family. And she also seemed ashamed to speak. "Oh, Mr. Revere, I'm sorry, indeed I am, but Mrs. Newberry has changed her mind about that silver bracelet she ordered. She doesn't want it made."

"I haven't begun it."

The young lady looked about and then spoke in a whisper. "She's angry about the bells not ringing, as mad as a wet hen. She said your son was to blame."

"He was, I'm sure he was."

"Then he's a grand boy and that was a grand deed. But I don't dare to say it when my mistress is around."

After she left, other servants came to cancel other orders. Some Tory men came themselves.

They had found they didn't need shoe buckles. Others decided they didn't want those snuffboxes and pocketbook clasps.

And so on and so on all day long. By late afternoon there was no work ahead.

"What will we do, Father?" Paul asked.

"I'll have to think about it. But don't tell your mother. There's no use to worry her now."

"I won't tell anyone."

YOUNG ENOUGH TO JUMP

That evening, at supper, Mrs. Revere said it was time to paint the house again. She had seen a painter and he would come tomorrow to make a price for the work.

"And, Father," said Debbie, "I really should have a new dress. I'm going up to Lexington to visit Cousin Sallie, you know."

"I'm afraid you can't have a new dress. And, Deborah, I'm sorry but the house can't be painted now."

Everyone but Paul was surprised. What was wrong? They had heard Mr. Revere say he wanted the house painted.

And he never refused to get new dresses for his daughters. He wanted them to look nice.

Paul wondered what his father would do. Would he tell them about the canceled orders? Paul wasn't certain.

Mr. Revere did tell them but not once did he blame Paul.

"It's my fault!" Paul exclaimed. "I should have rung the bell."

"No, no!" cried his mother. "I'm glad you refused, even if this house is never painted."

"I'm glad too!" cried Debbie. "I don't care if
I never have a new dress!"

"Never mind, Paul," said his father. "If we
can't work with silver we will work with iron."
he declared.

"Iron!" exclaimed the others.

Mr. Revere nodded. "We'll make things poor
folks can afford to buy. We'll make iron hinges,
bolts, hooks, and keys. We'll make pokers, tea-
kettles, and all such things."

"That's a big jump, from silver to iron," said
Mrs. Revere.

"Well, I'm still young enough to jump pretty
far," he replied.

The others laughed. Things weren't so bad if
Father could joke.

Paul was so happy he made up a verse. He
spoke it, too, then and there.

"Now iron is hard but iron is cheap;
Poor folks like us can buy a heap
Of pokers, hinges, bolts and rings,
And customers will come on wings."

"I like your verse, Paul," said his father. "It tells the truth. I believe people will buy a 'heap' of useful things. I'm sure I'll make a living."

AT THE SIGN OF THE IRON KEY

The very next day Mr. Revere and Paul took down the old sign that hung in front of the shop. On this was painted a coin bag with coins falling from it. Everyone in Boston knew what that meant—a silversmith shop.

Now they put up a new sign. On this was painted a huge iron key. And there was no need to explain what this meant. Everyone knew they could buy ironware there.

Business was good from the first. Boston was

growing fast. Every day ships brought people from Europe. The newcomers needed houses. Houses needed many things made of iron.

The newcomers told one another they could find everything at the Sign of the Iron Key. And the prices weren't too high, either. Before long Mr. Revere was making a good living.

The house couldn't be painted just yet and Debbie couldn't have a fancy dress. But the younger children could go to school, and that took some money. There were no free schools and no free schoolbooks.

Every morning, then, a little before seven o'clock, five younger Reveres left the house.

They were Frances, Thomas, John, Mary and Betty. And some were light and some were dark, but all were lively and gay.

Paul no longer went to fine houses to deliver silver. He had more time in the evenings.

Often he went to look at the Worthington's

wrought-iron gate. It seemed more beautiful to him now that he was working with iron.

Reginald had gone back to London so there was no danger of meeting him. Paul could gaze at the gate as long as he pleased.

After one of these visits, he wrote a verse:

> "I'm only iron, an old iron band,
>   But, use me with an artist's hand,
>   I'll turn into vines with a fancy whirl,
>   I'll turn into leaves with stems a-curl,
>   I'll turn into lace so very fine
>   'Twould be fit to use in a palace of thine.
>   In me great things of beauty hide;
>   Find them, artist, or ill betide."

Paul wished he could find these "things of beauty." Maybe he would be this "artist" himself sometime.

Will Indians Attack Boston?

AGAIN THE people of Boston feared an Indian attack. Bands of warriors had begun to burn farmers' houses and barns. A settlement was now in ashes from flaming arrows.

And these things happened not many miles from Boston. Would the Indians attack the city? The people were alarmed.

"You can't trust an Indian," a man declared. "That chief made a treaty of peace with the Governor of Massachusetts last year."

"And they have broken it already," another man said. "They kill and burn on the frontier now. They'll attack Boston next."

"I doubt that," still another citizen said. "They would be afraid to attack our company of militiamen."

"You are wrong, sir," a hunter put in. "The warriors outnumber our militamen. I discovered their camp last week while I was hunting near the Indian camp."

"Did you count the warriors?" a boy asked.

"I could tell by the size of their camp. It was large enough for a thousand."

"That is twice the number of militiamen we have," a woman said.

"Had the warriors painted their faces for war?" another woman asked the hunter.

"They had, ma'am, and they had a war dance every night. I was hiding close by and I watched them. I even heard a speech the chief made to his warriors."

"Did he urge them to attack Boston?" the first citizen asked.

"He did, sir. He got them so excited they were in a frenzy. I don't think he could hold them back if he tried."

"I was wrong when I said the braves wouldn't attack Boston," the first citizen confessed. "I believe they will. We must help our troops, men. We can all do guard duty. We're not too old for that."

"Aye!" a man cried. "Every man who can carry a gun must serve."

"Aye! Aye!" cried the other men. Then they all hurried away to get their guns ready.

"What will we do when the Indians come?" a young girl asked her mother. "Will we hide in our cellar?"

"No, Lucy, we'll go to the nearest church. Our governor has advised the people to do that whenever they are in danger."

"Even if they are not members?" her teenage daughter asked.

"Yes, Carrie. We don't belong to the nearest church, but that's where we will go. We'll be safer there than anywhere else."

"I think that's silly," her young son said. "Indians don't care anything about a church. They'd just as soon burn that down as a barn."

"Armed men will guard every church in Boston, John," his mother replied. "We may be protected by those very men who were here just a few minutes ago."

"I hope they are all sharp-shooters," John said. "That's what I'm going to be when I grow up," he vowed.

"If you live that long," his mother said sadly to herself.

Then they also hurried away.

Early the next morning, town criers went through every part of Boston. Each one rang his hand bell and shouted words that could be heard a mile away.

96

"Hark, people, hark! Indians! Go to nearest church! Take quilts and food! Hurry!"

THE CROWD IN OLD NORTH CHURCH

In a few minutes people were pouring from mansions, cottages, and tenements. The crooked streets and alleys were crowded with merchants, workers, and thieves. People hurried to the nearest church with their families.

The Reveres were on their way to the Old North Church with their bundles. Mr. Revere carried his valuable sheets of melted silver. They were hidden in the folds of a quilt.

"It's our bread and butter," he had told his family. "I can't leave them for Indians."

Debbie and Frances carried baskets of food. They also took care of the younger children.

Mrs. Revere had a bundle of medicines and a big roll of linen for bandages. "There may be flying arrows. Someone may be hurt," she had said. "We must be prepared."

Paul had his father's handsome silver pieces. The cups, mugs, buckles, thimbles, and rings were in one bundle. A silver tea set was in another. All were hidden in the folds of quilts.

Suddenly he noticed that his mother was weeping. He joined her at once and walked with her. "What's the matter, Mother?" he asked. "Are you frightened?"

"Not for myself, Paul. My tears are for Cousin Martha Hitchbourn. She is out on her farm alone. Her house is on the Boston road. The Indians will pass it."

"She can't be alone," Paul said. "Her four farm hands will be with her. They'll take her to the woods and hide."

"She might not be willing to leave her house. She's stubborn. The hands wouldn't have time to argue with her. They'd have to save themselves."

"It might be like that, but she's smart. She'll hide someplace."

"She couldn't hide in her house. The Indians would burn it, and her barn, too."

"The forest is close by," Paul suggested.

"But she'd have to cross a pasture to get there. She'd be afraid the Indians would see her."

"They would if they were near by. I'd hate to have anything happen to her, Mother."

"I know you would," Mrs. Revere replied. She said no more for they now reached the Old North Church.

Several armed citizens were guarding it. Their faces were grim and determined.

"It would take a good many savages to overcome them," the people told one another.

The Reveres found so many citizens inside they had trouble getting to their pew. They finally made it, however, and put their bundles under the benches.

"Some of us must watch all citizens every minute," Mr. Revere said softly. "There may be thieves among them."

"I'll be here," his wife replied. "You will want to talk with your friends. So will the older children, too."

"I'll take my turn later on," Paul said. Then he left the pew and almost at once was lost in the crowd. His family couldn't see him leave the church by the back door.

He had something to do and it must be done at once. He meant to save Cousin Martha. He was going for her now.

WILL PAUL BE TOO LATE?

Paul hurried toward the hitch rack to get a horse. "I'll have to take one without asking it's owner," he thought. "I've no time for that. I'll explain when I get back."

100

But a guard had a different idea. "Wait, young fellow!" he cried. "You're not planning to leave are you?" he asked.

"Well, yes. I have to go somewhere."

"You'll go nowhere. It's too dangerous."

Then Paul explained and the guard changed his mind. "You're a brave boy," he said. "And I'll help you to get away. You can ride my horse. It's saddled and bridled and ready to go."

"I don't want my family to know. They would be worried."

"I won't need to tell them or anyone. It's only two miles to the Hitchbourn farm. You can get there and back before anyone misses you. There's your horse, that black one."

"I'm much obliged, sir. Cousin Martha will want to thank you, too."

"I'm glad to help the lady," said the guard. "But I wouldn't let you go if I thought you would be in danger."

"Do you mean the Indians aren't coming after all?" Paul asked.

"No, indeed! Our scouts said they were far away just a little while ago. But Indians travel fast. So you must get your cousin here in a hurry."

Paul jumped to the saddle, saluted the guard, and rode away. He galloped nearly all the way to the Hitchbourn farm.

When he reached the house he dismounted and tied his horse to the hitch rack. Then he knocked loudly on the front door.

His cousin didn't answer, so he knocked again. Still the door wasn't opened.

Now he called out his name, "I'm Paul! Paul Revere, Cousin Martha!"

The door was opened by a lovely woman his mother's age. "Paul!" she cried. "Oh, I am glad to see you! Come in!"

The minute Paul was inside, his Cousin Martha closed the door and bolted it. The room was dark. Every window blind was down and no lamp was lighted.

"I thought an Indian was knocking," Martha said. "I'm glad you called your name. Sit down, Paul. You must be tired."

"There isn't time, Cousin Martha. I came to take you to Boston."

"My hands wanted me to go there with them. But they wouldn't wait for me to pack my china, and silver, and clothes."

"Neither will I," Paul said firmly. "We must hurry. Get your bonnet and shawl while I saddle your horse."

"Won't I have time to get my keepsakes?"

"You'll get nothing. Lock your doors and wait on your front steps."

He ran to the stable and saddled a horse quickly. He drove the other horse out and fastened the door so they couldn't go back.

"They'll run to the woods when they hear the Indians yelling. It will frighten them," he thought to himself.

He led his cousin's horse to the front steps and found her waiting there. She was about to mount when a scout from the militia rode up. "You can't go on the road now," he said. "The Indians are close and the militia is almost here. Go inside and bolt your doors. I'll hide your horses."

He waited until Martha and Paul went in the house. Then he rode away leading the horses.

Martha and Paul sat in the dark room and waited. They were too worried to talk. Each one was thinking about the battle that would soon be fought. Each one prayed the militia would win.

Suddenly they heard savage yells near by. Then came the welcome sounds of pipes and drums. The Boston militia was passing by!

In a few minutes there was gunfire and savage yells. Then more gunfire, volley after volley. This was followed by silence.

"Our troops won!" Martha cried. "I'll roll up the blinds. We'll go to the gate and wave to the militiamen as they go back."

"Wait till we hear their pipes and drums," Paul suggested. "Then we can be sure they won."

Presently they heard pipers piping merrily, and drummers drumming loudly.

"They won!" Paul cried. "Come on, Martha!"

They stood at the gate and waved as the troops passed by. Then the scout brought their horses back, and they rode behind the militia all the way to Boston.

The King and the Fish

A YEAR had passed. Paul was sixteen and handsomer than ever.

Now came another big event. Down came the Sign of the Iron Key and up again went the Sign of the Silver Coins!

Mr. Revere had jumped back into silversmithing. There were good reasons for the change.

Too many houses had been built: no more were needed just now.

Also no settlers were coming from England. There was fear of another Indian war. They had heard about the warriors running way from the Boston militia.

"But the Indians will keep on burning frontier settlements," Englishmen said.

Many wanted to move to America but not till Indian wars were over.

All this ruined Mr. Revere's trade. No one wanted keys, hinges, bolts and nails. He would have to go into some other business.

Then, just in the nick of time, his old Tory customers began to come back.

They hadn't been able to find a silversmith who could do beautiful work like Mr. Revere's.

They seemed to have forgotten the funeral. Or they pretended they had. The orders came so fast Mr. Revere had to get two new apprentices.

The shop was a busy place now. All day long there was the *rat-tat-tat* of little hammers on the silver metal.

This morning, however, there wasn't the sound of a single tap when Mr. Revere came at seven.

He was surprised. "I gave those boys work, and told them what to do last night."

He opened the door. Then he had another surprise. Not a boy was working!

Paul was holding up a large sheet of drawing paper. Joe and Henry were looking at it and grinning from ear to ear. None of them heard Mr. Revere enter.

"Did you make the drawings?" asked Joe.

"Of course." Paul nodded.

"See how big he made the king's feet, Henry! They look like barges," laughed Joe.

"Look at the king's hand, Joe! It's exactly like a lobster's claw," chuckled Henry.

"I wrote the verses, too," said Paul. "Listen, I'll recite them for you."

> "Now hark, you men of the fishing fleet!
> On you are resting the royal feet.
> Your fish he holds in his royal hand;
> Try to get one—you will be tanned.

"His shoes may be satin,
The heels low and light;
You'll think they are barges—
You'll have no chance to fight.

His hand is a claw,
Bony and weak.
But it holds all your fish—
You can't even squeak.

"Oh, would those royal feet were mine!
And would those royal hands were thine!
Your nets with fish would all run over,
And you yourselves would be in clover."

"Ha, ha, ha, ha!" shouted the boys and Paul laughed with them.

"How did you ever happen to think of it?" asked Joe when he was able to speak.

"I heard some fishermen talking yesterday. They were angry about the new 'Fish Law.'"

"Give me that paper!" said Mr. Revere sternly as he came forward.

Paul was surprised to hear his father's voice. "Oh! I didn't know you were here, Father."

"I heard you read the rhymes," Mr. Revere replied sternly.

"I wrote them late last night. I didn't have a chance to show them to you."

He gave the paper to his father, and Mr. Revere looked at it, but he didn't laugh.

"The governor would put you in jail for this," he said gravely. "You have made fun of the king and that is against the law. He is our ruler, you know, even if he is across the ocean."

"I just wrote it for fun."

"It's dangerous fun, Paul."

"The boys won't tell——"

"I won't," declared Henry.

"I won't," promised Joe.

"If you do, this shop will be closed and we'll all go to jail. The governor won't laugh at these rhymes. He knows he'll have trouble with the fishermen."

"I don't blame them," said Paul. "This new law forbids them to sell their salted fish in England. They say they'll starve if they can't."

"There are not enough people here to buy their catch," said Mr. Revere. "Not even if the Tories would buy."

"That's just it! They don't know what to do."

"It's a bad situation. There's no telling what will happen. But no matter how we feel about it, Paul, we can't make fun of the king."

"I'm sorry, Father."

Mr. Revere folded the sheet of paper and put it in his jacket pocket. Then he said it was time to get to work.

Presently nothing was heard in the smithy but the *rat-tat-tat* of hammers on silver metal.

Too Many Copies

By noon that day it was very hot. Mr. Revere and Paul carried their jackets when they went home to dinner. They hung them on wall pegs in the kitchen, dining, living room. They left them there when they went back to the shop.

Debbie and Frances cleared the table and washed the dishes. Then Debbie picked up a sheet of paper from the floor under the jackets.

She spread it out, looked at it and smiled. "It's some of Paul's verses," she cried. "His name is signed."

"It fell from his jacket pocket, I suppose," said Frances.

Debbie didn't answer. She was reading the verses to herself and laughing all the time.

"He wrote something funny again, didn't he? Please read them to me, Debbie."

Her sister read the verses aloud and Frances laughed. "Wouldn't that make old King George mad!" she exclaimed.

"It wouldn't make any patriot mad," Debbie replied. "Mother will love it. I'll give it to her when she comes back from the quilting party."

"Our relatives will like it, too," Frances added. "All of the Hitchbourns are patriots, too, you know."

"I'll make a copy for them."

Before long the relatives were making copies from Debbie's copy. Every Hitchbourn loved it, from eight years old to ninety.

Mr. Revere was away on business while this was going on. When he was told, upon his return, he didn't like it. "Too many copies are being

114

passed around," he said. "If a Tory should happen to see one, it will make trouble for Paul."

"How could it?" his wife asked. "Paul didn't sign the copies."

"But he did, Mother," Debbie put in. "All the relatives asked him to sign his name."

"Then we can expect a lot of trouble," her father declared.

"I don't see why we should," Debbie said. "Everyone promised to be careful."

"And no Hitchbourn would ever dream of showing Paul's verses to a Tory," said Deborah Hitchbourn Revere.

"We can only hope that no Hitchbourn will lose his copy," Mr. Revere replied. "Men and boys have been put in jail for saying less about the king than Paul did in his verses."

But alas for Mr. Revere and Paul a copy was lost. It was now in the mansion of the Tory shipbuilder, William Fuller.

"I found it on the street," the cook told his ten-year-old daughter, Annie. "I thought you would like to read it. It's funny."

Annie did like it. She read the verses three times and laughed every time. She didn't know what it meant and neither did the cook.

Annie took the copy to her mother. "It's funny," she said. "You'll laugh."

Mrs. Fuller didn't laugh. She frowned. "Where did you get this?" she asked.

"The cook found it on the street this morning."

Mr. Fuller came into the room. "William!" she cried, "just listen to this!" Then she read the verse aloud.

"Who wrote that?" he asked angrily.

"The name is Paul Revere."

"He's the son of the silversmith on Fish Street. I've seen the boy in the shop. Mr. Revere is a well-known patriot. These verses show that his son is just like him."

116

"Wasn't it funny what he wrote about the king's big feet?" asked Annie.

"Didn't you know he was making fun of our king, child?"

Annie shook her head. Her father went on.

"We can't allow anyone to ridicule our great ruler. This Paul Revere must be punished."

"Will that stop him from writing other verses like these?" Mrs. Fuller asked.

"I'll find a way to stop him! He'll never write another line."

PAUL'S PUNISHMENT

Paul Revere didn't dream he was being followed. It was lucky for him that he didn't deliver the silverware anymore. The apprentices did that now. Paul had become an engraver and seldom left the shop.

When he did, he was always with his friends,

117

the bellringers. He swam, and walked, and rode with them often.

The spy reported this to Mr. Fuller. "The boy is never alone," he said. "I've had no chance to seize him."

"Then we'll try another plan," Mr. Fuller said. "I will go to the Revere shop in the morning. I will tell the smith that my wife likes his son's engravings. And that she wishes him to engrave her plain silver pieces. He must come to my house that evening to see about this."

"That should do it, sir. Shall I wait till he enters your yard?"

"No. Seize him in the first dark place on Fish Street, and take him down to my cargo boat. It is being loaded now and will sail for England tomorrow night."

Paul was delighted with Mr. Fuller's message. Of course he'd go. He might get a big order.

It was a handsome young silversmith who left

his home that evening. He was too happy to mind the black dark of Fish Street.

Suddenly he was seized by two men. He tried to get away. "Help!" Help!" he shouted.

Then he was hit on the back of his neck. It was a hard blow and he fell unconscious.

When he came to, he was lying on a bunk in a tiny room. His hands and feet were tightly tied with ropes. He tried to free his hands, but he had to give up.

He knew that he was on a ship. He could smell the waters of the bay. He was so frightened he began to sob.

Now the boat's Tory captain entered. "You'd better save your tears. You'll need them when you're in a London prison."

"London!" Paul exclaimed. "Why are you taking me there?"

"You made fun of our king. Isn't that reason enough? You'll never see Boston again—never so long as you live." He left then and closed the door with a bang.

Paul was terrified. "I'll never see my folks again," he thought.

A young American sailor slipped quietly into Paul's room. He spoke to Paul hurriedly.

"I'll save you boy. I'm a patriot myself. You can thank that Tory shipbuilder for this. I heard him tell the captain to take you to England and put you in prison."

Now Paul was free. He stood and tried to thank the young man.

"S-sh!" the sailor whispered. "You're not safe yet." He opened the door and looked out. "All clear! Jump overboard from the stern. You can swim can't you?"

"Like a fish," Paul said. "And thanks again, Patriot." Then he hurried away.

The sailor waited and listened. When he heard a big splash, he smiled and went forward.

Riot and Rescue

PAUL WAS SAFE at home now. And he was delighted to see his verses coming true. The fishermen were trying to get rid of the king's royal feet and hands.

There was a riot on the fisherman's wharf this morning. Fishermen fought English soldiers and were arrested.

Then a hundred fishermen came running from the shore and freed the prisoners. It was so sudden the soldiers had no time to fire. The fishermen threw them into the sea.

By the time they got out every fisherman had disappeared.

Paul told his family all about it at supper. He had seen the whole thing. He had followed the soldiers to the wharf.

"Of course they got away," said Mr. Revere. "Every patriot in Boston would help them. A door is opened quietly—the street is dark and narrow—a door closes quietly and a fisherman is safe."

"I'm glad Cousin Ben Hitchbourn is away fishing," said Mrs. Revere. "He would have been in the thick of the fight."

"Come to think of it, Deborah, it's about time for him to come back with his catch. Boston will be a dangerous place for any fisherman just now," her mother said.

"He's likely to be arrested. They'll take his boat, too, and he can't afford to lose it. Can't we warn him?" Deborah asked.

"I wish we could, but every road will be guarded tonight. They'll be watching for fishermen trying to leave town. A man would need a mighty good reason to be out tonight. I'd be afraid to try."

"I can warn him," said Paul. "I know where his camp is. I've been there a dozen times. It's at May's Point."

"The guards would stop you the same as they would your father. If he had no excuse for being out, neither would you."

"But, Mother, Father never delivers his work anymore. I could be taking something to someone out that way."

"That's the very thing!" exclaimed Mr. Revere. "I've just finished some gold knee buckles for Mr. Arnold on the Lexington Pike."

"And I can deliver them! Why, it will be easy. I know the country, too. I couldn't get lost if I tried. Besides, these English soldiers don't know our back roads and short cuts."

"They couldn't know," his father said. "The

124

governor sent for them only one month ago. They are his special guard."

"You see, Mother," Paul went on, "I'll ride on the Pike as far as Mr. Arnold's. Then I'll cut through to the coast. It's moonlight and I can see the paths."

"It sounds all right," admitted Deborah. "But what about Indians?"

"There aren't any up there near the coast," said Mr. Revere. "There haven't been for years. There are too many farms."

"Yes, and the woods are nothing but groves. The underbrush is all cut out," declared Paul.

"I believe he can make it, Deborah. He isn't even taking a chance. He is out on an errand for his master. He knows the country."

"That's true——"

"If guards do stop him he can talk his way out. Paul is very good at that. He can make things seem as though they aren't."

Deborah smiled. "I know that too well. All right, Paul. Go ahead. I'll get an early breakfast for you."

"I'm going now, Mother. The guards may not be out. They won't expect the fishermen while the moon is so bright."

"That's true. A man running away waits for the dark," said his father. "Get Rex saddled at once and I'll bring the buckles to the stable."

Mr. Revere went to the shop and Paul started out the door.

"I wish you had time to call on Cousin Martha, Paul. She lives just this side of the Arnold farm."

"Yes, I know, but I won't have time. Goodby, Mother! I'm off!"

A Moonlight Ride

OLD BOSTON was nearly surrounded by water. There was only one place where anyone could get out of the city by land. This was by way of the mud flats.

This place was called "The Neck" because it was so narrow.

Paul worried about this place as he rode toward it. Guards might be here. It was such a good place to stop travelers.

He planned what he would say to them and what they would say to him.

He would show them the buckles and they would tell him to ride on.

Sure enough, two English soldiers on horses were waiting at the Neck. He saw them plainly in the bright moonlight.

They stopped him and asked him why he was leaving Boston at night.

He explained he had to deliver a package out on Lexington Pike. Then he showed the gold buckles. All this was just as he had planned. From then on it was different.

The soldiers accused him of stealing the buckles. They said he was running away and they might arrest him for theft.

Paul said he could prove he was a silversmith's apprentice and that his master had given him the buckles. They could go to his shop on Fish Street and ask Mr. Revere.

"Well, anyway," said one, "you're one of those fishermen. You were in that riot on the wharf and you can't deny it!"

"I do deny it!" exclaimed Paul. "Can't you

take my word for anything? I'm not a fisher-man," he declared hotly.

"You might be carrying a message to the ring-leader," the other soldier said.

Paul was angry now and talked too much for his good. He said there weren't any ringleaders. At least he didn't see any and he was on the wharf.

"Oh! So you were on the wharf! He con-fesses it, Bill. That proves he's one of them."

Paul tried to explain that he had followed the soldiers because he just wanted to see what was going on.

They wouldn't listen to him. They made him dismount and went through his pockets.

Paul wasn't worried, he knew they wouldn't find any written messages. The only message he carried was in his head, for Ben.

But now again things went wrong. Bill found a folded paper in Paul's jacket pocket. Then the boy knew he was in trouble. He was wearing his father's jacket. Bill had found his verses about the king.

The soldier read them without a smile. "So that's the kind of stuff you carry about!" he exclaimed. "Did you write this?"

"Yes, sir, but it was just for fun."

"You make fun of His Majesty King George, do you? This will certainly put you in jail, young man."

By this time the other soldier had read it and he also was indignant. "I think it's a secret message," he said. "They've drawn the big feet and fish to make it look funny and innocent. But they can't deceive me."

"Me neither, Ed. I think it's as you say. Let's go to this Arnold's with him. Maybe we'll find out something."

"Mount your horse and lead the way," Paul was ordered.

130

He obeyed. He was really alarmed now, not so much for himself as for Mr. Arnold.

His father had told him a secret about Mr. Arnold while he was saddling Rex.

"You must know it now, Paul," his father had said. "You may see things you won't understand when you stop at the Arnold farm. But you will keep this secret—I can trust you."

Then his father told him that Silas Arnold often hid patriots on his farm. These men had done no wrong, but they would be put in jail if the governor's guards ever could find them.

"It is likely," he went on "that several fishermen are hiding there now. If you should see them you must not tell anyone, not even your cousin Ben."

"No one can make me tell on a patriot like Mr. Arnold," Paul had said. And now here he was, leading enemy soldiers right to this very patriot's home.

He wouldn't do it! How could he get out of it? He thought hard as he rode ahead of them.

They were coming closer to Mr. Arnold's farm and still he didn't know what to do.

Then he had an idea! If it worked, these men wouldn't even see Mr. Arnold's farm.

He would pretend that Cousin Martha's farm was Arnold's. She lived just a mile this side. They wouldn't know the difference.

But then he would have to pretend that Martha was Mrs. Arnold and that Mr. Arnold was her husband.

And Cousin Martha didn't have a husband. She wasn't married.

Would she let him say she was? "She never told a lie about anything," his mother had said. "She thinks it's a sin to tell a little fib."

Paul remembered this as they came to the Hitchbourn farm. They would be at the house in two minutes.

132

Well, he'd try it. That was the only way he could save Mr. Arnold and also the fishermen hiding there.

He stopped his horse. "Here is the house," he said softly.

"Dismount and knock," said Bill. "Don't go inside. I'll hold your horse."

Paul went up the two steps and knocked at the door. He was so excited now, he was trembling. His knees shook, he was icy cold. He thought the door would never open. He hoped it wouldn't.

But it did and there in the hall stood Miss Martha Hitchbourn.

WHAT DID MARTHA SAY?

Martha was astonished. She looked at Paul. She looked at the two British soldiers. She noticed Paul's pale and worried face.

She suspected the boy was in trouble. She was sure of it when he spoke to her.

"Good evening, Madam," he said.

Martha was astonished but she didn't show it. She was too smart.

If Paul wanted to pretend she was a stranger before these British soldiers, there was a good reason for it.

"All right," she said to herself. "I'll be a stranger. These Tories won't get anything out of me."

"Well!" she said aloud, sharply. "Who are you? What are you doing here this time of night?" she demanded.

"I came to deliver the knee buckles your husband ordered."

"My what?"

Paul pretended she was deaf. "Your husband!" he shouted. "His knee buckles from Revere, the silversmith!"

Martha's face turned red, then white. She just stood there and looked at Paul. It was a full moment before she spoke.

It was the longest moment he had ever known. What would she say?

If he could only tell her that her answer could save patriots from prison!

If he could only warn her that Silas Arnold's life depended on her words!

But he couldn't. The guards were so close they could hear a whisper.

Then, at last, Martha spoke and her voice was sharp and angry. "I must say you took your time about it. Why didn't you bring them a month ago as you promised?"

"Uh—uh——" Paul gasped. "We—we were very busy then."

"You'd better learn to keep your word. It would serve your master right if my husband refused to take them."

"Mr. Revere will be sorry——"

"Sorry! Humph! Little good that will do. My husband has needed these buckles. He wanted to wear them today when he went to Nantucket Island," Martha replied.

"Yes, ma'am——"

"Now be off with you and tell your master every word I said."

"Yes, ma'am." Paul turned away.

"Stay! I've changed my mind. I'll pay for them now, but you'll have to wait till I can remember where I hid the money."

Then she turned to the guard.

"Is that why you came along?" she asked. "Was Mr. Revere afraid we wouldn't pay? I never was treated like this before in all my life. Never! We don't owe a penny to anyone. My husband is an honest man, I'll have you know.

"It's an insult!" she went on. "My husband will be good and angry when he hears about it."

"Oh, for goodness sake!" exclaimed Bill.

"Let's get out of here, Ed. Looks as though she's wound up for the night. Let the boy stay."

Bill gave Paul his reins and told him to wait for his money.

They galloped away and Paul followed his cousin into the narrow hall.

Martha bolted the hall door. She drew the thick curtain across the window.

"Cousin Martha," Paul began.

"S-sh!" Martha placed her finger on her lips and motioned Paul to follow her.

She led him into the large kitchen where a fire was burning in the fireplace.

"Now," she said, "we'll sit here by the fire and talk. But speak softly. They might come back and eavesdrop. Now then, tell me everything you know."

Paul told her everything.

"I knew something was wrong the minute I

saw your face. And you were right about the fishermen. Several went to the Arnold farm. They stopped here to ask the way."

"I was so afraid—that is, I didn't know what you would say about a husband," Paul stammered nervously.

"I told a lie; I can never again say I am a Puritan."

"You can say you're a patriot. The family will be proud of you."

There was silence for a moment. Then Martha laughed merrily. "How I did carry on!" she exclaimed. "I didn't know it was in me."

"I didn't either."

Then they both laughed and laughed about Cousin Martha's husband and his knee buckles.

At Ben's Fishing Camp

PAUL DIDN'T leave his cousin's home till daybreak. She had made him go to bed. "You're all fagged out," she said. "And you show it. You've had too many worries."

After a good beakfast he started for the camp at May's Point. But he kept away from roads. He cut through pastures and groves, rode in creek beds and all the time rode slowly.

His father had cautioned him, "Don't ride fast: some Tory will suspect you and tell the guards."

Finally he reached the coast and now here was May's Point and his cousin's camp. He didn't expect to find anyone there this time of the day. They would be out in the boat fishing.

But here they were on the shore, all six of them. They were busy mending a big net.

Ben saw him as he tied Rex and came running to greet him. He loved this young cousin. The boy was smart and trustworthy.

Paul loved his older cousin, too. Ben was big and jolly and kind. All his men loved him.

"Well, 'pon my word, here's Paul, boys!" Ben shouted. "Here's Paul!"

The others came running. They all knew Paul and were glad to see him.

He hated to tell them about the new Fish Law. It would make them unhappy.

"You should have come sooner," Ben was saying. "We'll be sailing to Boston tomorrow."

"We've had good luck, Paul," said Samuel Bowen.

"Best catch we've ever had," said Nate Green.

141

"We'll all make a bit of money this time," declared William Hudson. "I'll have enough to send my children to school."

"I'm going to repair my house," said Charles Lyons. "It's about to fall down."

"I'll make a larger fireplace," said John Lewis. "We nearly froze last winter."

Now Paul hated more than ever to tell them, but it had to be done. "I've brought bad news!" he exclaimed. "There's been trouble in Boston."

The men listened while Paul told them about the new law and the riot. He explained he had come to warn them of the danger of their arrest if they were seen in Boston now. He told about the guards stopping him and how they let him go because of the knee buckles.

He didn't tell what happened at Martha's. Nor that he had the buckles in his pocket now and would deliver them to Mr. Arnold on his way home. All this was part of the secret.

142

He did tell them about his verses and how angry the soldiers were when they read them.

"They hate us patriots," said Samuel.

"Yes," nodded Ben, "they do. That's another reason we must stay away from Boston until this thing blows over."

Then there was silence. Each man wondered how he could keep his family this winter. Jobs were scarce now. There wasn't much a man could do for a living, except fish.

"Well, Ben," said William, "I guess we might as well dump our catch into the ocean."

"Aye!" the other said.

"Wait a minute," Ben advised. "There's no hurry about dumping. There are other places we can sell fish besides England. What about salted fish for Cuba?"

"Cuba! Of course! Cuba!" they cried. Then sad faces brightened. They jumped to their feet and laughed and patted Ben on his back. They said that they could start at daybreak if he was willing.

"We'll have to go at once," he answered, "if we get there before another new Fish Law is made. His Majesty will probably declare we can't trade in Cuba next."

"He will!" exclaimed Samuel. "I've no doubt of that. He does everything he can against us."

"I can't understand him," said John. "He claims this country and he says we are his subjects. And yet he won't help us."

"He wants to punish us because we are Americans, I guess," said Nate.

"No," said Ben, "it's because so many of us are patriots."

"That's it! That's it!" agreed the others.

"I wish you could go to Cuba with us, Paul," said Ben.

"I wish I could. But Father said I could stay overnight with you if you wanted me."

"If we wanted you!" exclaimed his cousin. "Why, bless your heart, the camp is yours!"

"Aye! Aye!" cried the others earnestly.

"You see how we feel about you, Paul. You're a brave boy to take such a long and dangerous ride to warn us.

"Every one of us is thankful to you."

YARNS AROUND THE CAMPFIRE

The rest of the day was spent getting the boat ready for the long voyage to Cuba.

Paul helped carry the supplies and clothing aboard. He helped haul in the heavy fish net. He helped whenever he was needed. He even helped get the supper. He could broil fish as well as anyone, he said. And after the fishermen tasted it they agreed with him.

After supper they sat around a big campfire and rested.

145

Presently Ben remembered Paul's verses and asked him to recite them.

The men were delighted. They were all young and devoted patriots. So they enjoyed making fun of the king. In fact they enjoyed it so much they made Paul repeat the poem until they had learned it themselves. Then they were all reciting it, Ben with the rest.

After a while they settled down to hear William's good old sea monster story.

"I didn't think much about this monster the first time I saw it," William began. "It came pretty close to the boat, I noticed. Then I forgot all about it. But when it came the next evening at the same time, I took a good look. And sure as I'm sitting here, that serpent lifted its head high right up over the deck rail. Then it looked straight at me and sneezed."

"My, my!" cried Ben. "It really sneezed?"

"It's a fact. And that's not all. It did the same

thing three nights running. It looked straight at me and sneezed. Of course I knew it was warning us of a storm."

"Of course," the men agreed solemnly.

"Good old serpent!" said Ben. "Did you trim your sails for the wind?"

"We did and that was all that saved us. And when I lay me down to sleep I always thank that serpent for that sneeze."

"Amen!" said the fishermen solemnly.

Paul laughed heartily. He not only enjoyed the story, he enjoyed the way the men poked fun at it.

"Now, it's our turn, Sam," said Ben. "Paul hasn't heard your 'Codfish Bridge' story."

"Oh, yes, that one," nodded Samuel. "Well, one day we ran into a school of cod so thick we couldn't sail through. No matter which way you looked you couldn't see a thing but cod, millions of 'em.

"We couldn't go on; we couldn't go back; we couldn't tack; we couldn't do anything. So, we jest used 'em for a bridge and walked over to the land."

"Well! Well!" exclaimed some.

"We carried a skiff and some food," Sam went on. "And we took blankets, of course."

"Of course!" said others, nodding.

"Well, we had to camp there for about a week before the cod ran out. And if we didn't see strange sights! One day six deer walked over 'em for a look at our ship. They walked back, too, and didn't get a hoof wet."

The men groaned; Sam paid no attention.

"Another day a big brown bear walked out on 'em for a mile or two. But she had a little trouble."

"What kind of trouble?" asked Paul.

"Well, sir, she ate so many she couldn't walk back. She had to roll."

The men laughed. This was the first time Sam had "rolled" the bear back to land.

"There was a lot of travel on that cod bridge. We saw cranes, gulls, lobsters, hawks, owls, weasels, foxes and walrus. And not one of them paid any attention to the others."

"Come, come," objected Nate. "Don't tell me a fox would let a nice fat gull go by."

"It's a fact, Nate. They were all too busy slipping and sliding. It was fun to watch them.

"But the funniest thing of all was the rabbit dance one night. The fish were too slick for them and every time they hopped they fell down and slid. There were a hundred or so, all big rabbits. And pretty soon they were sliding over one another and getting all tangled up in heaps. Well, sir, we had to go out and carry 'em over to land. Poor fellows, they seemed so grateful to us!"

"Even the ones you saved for breakfast?" asked Ben.

The men laughed. They always laughed at Sam's bridge story.

Of course Paul enjoyed it. After he went to bed he began to wish he were a fisherman. He'd be out in the open. He'd breathe the wonderful ocean air. He'd make up yarns and tell them. Wasn't that better than being shut up in a smithy? Wasn't it better than breathing the fumes of melting silver?

Then he thought of the king's new Fish Law and decided he'd rather be a silversmith.

A Great Surprise

AFTER AN EARLY breakfast the camp was deserted. The fishermen were on their boat and ready to sail away to Cuba.

Paul was on his horse and ready to go back to Boston. He was waving to his friends now. "Good-by! Good-by!" he called. Then he turned his horse toward the main highway.

It was almost noon when he reached Cousin Martha's farm, but he didn't stop. He had some corn-meal cakes left from last night's supper.

He was in a hurry to get home. His father needed him. Besides, they would all worry until they saw him and knew he was safe.

He had to stop at Mr. Arnold's to deliver the buckles and that might take some time. He might have trouble getting to see him.

He remembered the place. He had passed it many times, but he had never been inside the grounds.

The big frame house was quite a distance from the road. A long driveway led to it with trees on each side. The mansion itself was surrounded with stately elm trees and thick shrubbery. There was a large stable and big vegetable garden. There were fields and pastures.

Surrounding all this was a wood with so much underbrush it looked like a jungle. Paul had often wondered why this hadn't been cleared out. There were always workmen about and Mr. Arnold had plenty of money.

But now he didn't wonder. He knew why the jungle was left. It made a good hiding place.

He remembered also the gardener's cottage

at the entrance. The gardener probably watched the driveway and allowed no stranger to enter.

Well, if he couldn't get in he would take the buckles back to his father. He wouldn't give them to any gardener or anyone he didn't know. They were solid gold and very handsome. His father had engraved them with beautiful curved lines. This made them even more valuable.

Paul had come now to the Arnold farm. Here was the gate and it was closed.

Before he could dismount a man came from the cottage just inside the grounds. He asked Paul sharply what he wanted and who he was.

Paul gave him his name and that was enough. As soon as the man heard it he motioned him on. "Mr. Arnold is expecting you," he said.

This surprised Paul. Had his father sent a message? Had that Tory ship builder made trouble?

He was alarmed but he hitched his horse at

a post near the front porch, and prepared to meet Mr. Arnold. He dusted his clothing. He straightened his waistcoat. He was very particular with his hair and his three-cornered hat.

A neat-looking lad knocked at the wide white door a moment later. If he was worried he didn't show it.

Mr. Arnold himself opened the door and greeted Paul with a friendly smile. "You are Paul Revere," he said. "I have seen you in the shop. Come in, come in."

He led the way to his library and offered Paul a seat by the fire. But the boy did not take it. Instead he handed Mr. Arnold the package.

Mr. Arnold was very pleased with his buckles. He said the engraving was beautiful and that Mr. Revere was an artist.

He paid for them and Paul started out.

"Your cousin Martha came to see me this morning, Paul. She told me you would be here."

Then Mr. Arnold laughed heartily. "That was a good idea about Martha's 'husband.' I'm very grateful to you.

"You saved me from a lot of trouble. It would

have been very bad if the governor's guards had searched this place last night. I had too many guests I couldn't explain."

"Aren't the fishermen here now?"

"Only a few. The others went to another farm I own a few miles from here. All of them are now wood choppers.

"At least, no one can say they are not wood choppers. They are cutting down trees for me and will be paid for their work."

"May I tell my father this?"

"Yes, indeed. And by the way, one of my visitors knows your father and you also. Wouldn't you like to meet him?"

"I haven't much time. I must be getting back."

"It won't take long and he needs to see someone he knows. He's been in hiding some time and he's getting discouraged."

"Oh, then, I'll take the time."

"He's out in the wood. Come along, I'll show you where he's working."

IT WAS A FACE HE KNEW!

They passed through a clean stable yard. They passed by a big vegetable garden with its long straight rows of growing plants. They crossed a pasture and entered the wood.

The sound of chopping was near them now, quite near.

"There he is!" said Mr. Arnold. "Just go on alone. I'll see you when you leave."

Paul went on a little farther. Then he saw the chopper but he was bending over. Paul couldn't see his face. "Good day, sir," said Paul.

The chopper straightened and turned. Paul was so astonished he almost stopped breathing. It was a face he knew!

It was Mickey!

Then the boys were hugging each other and pounding each other on the back, and laughing and shouting, and almost crying too.

They sat on a log and Mickey told Paul what had happened to him.

"I came here that morning I left the tailor. I told Mr. Arnold how the man treated me, and he said he would hide me until my apprenticeship was ended."

"Why didn't you come to us, Mickey?"

"Your folks couldn't hide me in Boston. Your father would have been arrested if he had."

"I didn't know you knew Mr. Arnold. You never talked about him."

"I didn't think I should, even to you. He hid my father once when he couldn't pay his taxes."

"He's one of the finest patriots in Boston. I wish I could help our people, too," Paul said.

"I'm going to help them. As soon as my time is up I shall buy a little farm and hide patriots."

"I'll help you, Mickey. Here's my hand on it."

They shook hands just as they used to do so long ago.

Paul had to go now but he said he would come again soon.

Mr. Arnold was waiting at the gate. "I'm glad you saw Mickey," he said. "He gets tired of hiding. It was good for him to talk with a friend."

"It was good for me, too. Now I won't have to worry about him. He's safe here with you."

"Paul, I need someone to carry messages and I've been thinking of you. I may have to send a warning to my farm."

"A warning? I don't understand."

"Some Tory spy might find out about my visitors. Then soldiers would be sent to search both farms!"

"Those Tories are always spying on patriots."

"We have our spies, too. I receive information from them right along."

"How would it help to warn the men? If soldiers came wouldn't they find your visitors?"

"Not if they were warned in time. There are secret hiding places at both farms. The British guards would see only a few workers."

"I don't know whether Father will consent."

"And if he does?"

"I'll be glad to help. There's nothing I'd rather do."

"I shall ask him at once. You are just the kind of boy I need. You are brave and you have good common sense. You think quickly and you act quickly. And you are honest. I feel that I could trust you with any secret."

"I would never tell anything that would get a patriot into trouble."

"I know that. Mickey has told me many things about your devotion to the patriot cause.

"Good-by! You'll hear from me soon."

Secret Messages

MR. REVERE had consented. He told Mr. Arnold he would always spare Paul to carry messages. His work would have to get along somehow.

Two weeks had passed and nothing had happened. Paul was disappointed. He wanted a chance to see Mickey again but he'd have to wait till Mr. Arnold sent for him.

Then one morning a strange thing happened. Mr. Fogarty, the wharfmaster, came to the shop when Paul was there alone.

He closed the door carefully. He looked about carefully. Then he spoke to Paul in a very low voice.

162

"You must take a message to Silas Arnold at once, Paul. I overheard some British officers talking just now. They said——"

Mr. Fogarty stopped suddenly, for the door was opened and a customer came in.

This man was a Tory and a well-known one. Being polite, he waited for Mr. Fogarty to finish his business. Mr. Fogarty spoke to him politely, then turned back to Paul.

"I believe I shall leave a note for your father," he said. And this time he did not speak softly.

"I have changed my mind about the size of that silver mug I ordered."

Paul brought him ink and paper.

Mr. Fogarty thought a moment, then threw the pen down on the counter.

"I'll wait till I can talk with him. I'll come back later."

He left the shop quickly, and the other man took his place at the counter.

164

"When will your father return?"

"Not before an hour, sir."

"I want to see him about making a gold clasp for my pocketbook. I'll come back this afternoon."

Paul was glad to be alone. He wanted to think about Mr. Fogarty's words.

"You must take a message to Mr. Arnold at once," he had said.

How did he know Paul was to carry messages? He wouldn't know unless Mr. Arnold had told him.

That showed he was working with Mr. Arnold. He might even be a patriot spy. Of course! That's exactly what he was.

Then Paul wondered why Mr. Fogarty talked about a silver mug. Mr. Revere wasn't making a silver mug for him.

He probably said that so the Tory would think he was there on business.

And why did he leave his pen? Did he forget it or did he leave it on purpose?

Did it have something to do with the message for Silas Arnold?

He examined the quill closely. There was nothing unusual about it.

Its pearly white color was slightly darkened in places with ink stains. Most quill pens were.

No, he couldn't see anything different about this quill.

He was about to put it down when he discovered something. There *was* something unusual about it!

It was just a little too heavy. Perhaps there was something inside—a message!

He couldn't see anything. So he hurried to his workbench and came back with a long slender tool. He put this down into the quill carefully and felt something.

It was a tiny piece of paper!

166

He drew it out and examined it. There was writing on it, very fine small writing and a little hard to read.

This is what he saw:

"Warn S.A. Soldiers to search both farms today."

Paul put the paper back in the quill and thrust it in his pocket. He knew now what he must do and he must hurry.

He wrote a note to his father saying he had gone hunting. That was what Mr. Revere told him to say in case Mr. Arnold sent for him.

Then he hurried to the stable, saddled Rex and was on his way to the Neck.

British scouts were sure to be on the roads today. They would keep travelers off the main highway so the soldiers could ride quickly to the Arnold farms.

They would make carts and wagons turn into side roads. And droves of cattle would be driven off, of course.

Paul didn't think they would pay any attention to him jogging along at one side. If they did stop him he would say he was on an errand for his master. There was nothing strange about that in broad daylight.

But what errand? He must decide quickly before he reached the Neck. There might be guards at that place. There always were in times of trouble.

He hadn't thought to bring a silver piece, he could pretend to deliver. He must think of some other reason.

He could be out to collect money owed his master. But who owed this money? He'd have to be careful. Guards might go with him as they did before. This gave him an idea.

Why, he'd say Cousin Martha's husband owed

for those gold buckles. Of course! The very thing!

He was smiling about this and very pleased with himself as he came to the Neck.

PAUL ACTS QUICKLY

No guards at the Neck; no guards on the road; no British soldiers anywhere. Things were going well with young Paul Revere.

He began to think Mr. Fogarty had made a mistake.

He was only three or four miles now from Mr. Arnold's farm. With good luck he would be there soon.

He rode faster now; there was no one on the road but a few farmers. They wouldn't be suspicious; boys always rode faster than old men.

Suddenly he was stopped. Four British soldiers rode out of a side road just ahead and surrounded him. One was an officer and he did the talking. He asked Paul where he was going.

Paul said he was collecting money for his master. He was going to a certain farm.

"Why, that's the very lad I stopped one day!" cried a soldier. "He had a poem that made fun of the king. He wrote it himself, he said that he did."

"Oh!" exclaimed the officer. "So you are one of those patriots, are you?"

"Yes, sir."

"That settles it. Search him, boys."

He then ordered Paul to dismount but Paul did not obey. Instead he laughed.

"You'll find nothing on me, Sergeant, nothing but my quill pen. Here it is!"

He took the goose quill from his pocket.

"This is all. I give you my word."

"I didn't ask for your word," the officer said sharply. "Dismount!"

170

Paul was pleased with the way things were going. They paid no attention to the quill.

Now if his luck held out——

He sprang from his horse, held the quill in his mouth and lifted his arms to be searched.

"Nothing on him, Sergeant," said one soldier when the search was over.

"Ride on!" the officer ordered. "And you'd better not carry any messages to these rebels. You'll be caught sooner or later."

Paul mounted his horse. The soldiers left.

"Just by the skin of my teeth," muttered the boy. "Just by the skin of my teeth!"

BRITISH SOLDIERS ARE COMING!

A little later Paul stopped Rex at the big gate to the Arnold place.

The gardener came out at once and started to open the gate.

"No, no! Don't open it! British soldiers are
coming to search for patriots. They may come
any minute now. Here, take this quill to Mr.
Arnold. He will know what it means. I am go-

172

ing on to the upper farm. Tell Mr. Arnold I will warn the men there."

Then Paul galloped away and the gardener ran up the long drive toward the mansion.

Paul was afraid he would be stopped again. He feared British scouts might be spying near the other farm. What would he do if he found them at the gate?

If he saw them in time he would hide Rex in the brush and go on foot. He'd get inside through some field or pasture.

However, there were no scouts at the gate— only Mr. Arnold's watchman.

Again Paul was full of fear. Precious time would be lost while he explained his errand.

But Mr. Arnold had prepared for everything. As soon as Paul gave his name the gate was opened and he rode in.

"British soldiers are coming!" he cried. "I came to warn the patriots!"

"They are scattered through the woods," said the watchman. "Ride down that path. Call out as you go. They know what to do."

So down the path Paul Revere galloped calling out all the time, "British soldiers are coming! Hide! Hide! Patriots! They are coming to seize you! Hide, Patriots, hide!"

Now he was deep in the woods and a man waved at him and told him to stop.

Paul dismounted. The man took his horse away to hide it.

Other men came running and told Paul to follow them. They led him to a tangled wall of vines and bushes. They crawled through a small opening and the boy followed them.

To his surprise he was in a big cave. Other men came now and kept on coming until there were some ten.

No one spoke. It was so quiet the least noise outside could be heard.

174

The men sat on the ground and waited. They were all worried. They didn't know whether they were safe here. If some soldier discovered this cave they were lost. They would be dragged off to jail, every last one of them.

They sat silently and hoped and prayed.

It seemed hours to Paul before the soldiers came, but it was really only twenty minutes.

Then they heard British voices outside, and they knew the soldiers had come.

They heard them beating the bushes with clubs. Now the sounds were quite near; now they were far away. Presently they ceased altogether, but the men in the cave didn't move.

Again it seemed a long time to Paul before the watchman came. He was thankful when he heard the man's voice at the entrance.

"Come out, friends!" he called. "The soldiers have gone and the coast is clear."

Outside the cave the patriots gathered about

Paul and thanked him for his warning. They pressed his hand. They said they would never forget his loyalty to the patriot cause.

Paul stopped at Mr. Arnold's home on the way back. He found the patriots there had not been discovered either.

Again Paul was thanked for his warning.

"You are getting ahead of me, Paul," said Mickey. "You're already saving patriots and I haven't even bought my farm."

"I knew you'd make a splendid messenger," said Silas Arnold. "Don't be surprised if you're called on again."

Paul rode home with their praises ringing in his ears. It was great to help these patriots, he thought. It made him feel good inside. He hoped he would be sent again with messages.

"I'll carry them," he said aloud. "I'll get them there, too, just as sure as my name is Paul Revere."

176

A Centennial Celebration

It was nine o'clock in the morning on April 18, 1875.

People were coming from all parts of the big city of new Boston to the narrow winding streets of little old Boston.

They were all going to Christ Church, "the Old North."

Its eight bells were ringing joyously. A great celebration of a great event was to be held there this morning.

The church was filled now. People were standing at the door and in the yard, and still more people were coming.

Now the bells stopped ringing. The large audience was silent. A speaker stood on the platform and began to talk.

"This is the first one-hundred-year celebration of a great event, one of the greatest in American history—the midnight ride of Paul Revere.

"It was this ride that made Mr. Revere famous. For one hundred years people have talked about it and wondered at his courage.

"We are proud that he was born in Boston in 1735. He lived here all his life.

"We are proud, too, that he was not only the best silversmith in Boston, he was the best in America. Anyone who now owns a piece made by him treasures it highly. His work was beautiful and very artistic.

"However, it is not his skill as a silversmith that we are celebrating today. It is his patriotism, his great love for America.

"It led him to take this dangerous ride. It led

178

him to risk his life again and again by capture or even by death.

"It wasn't easy to be a patriot at that time: it wasn't even safe.

"Boston was filled with enemy soldiers. The barracks were crowded. They were quartered in the homes of citizens. There were two in the sexton's home here in our churchyard.

"On the night of April 18, 1775, some eight hundred of these soldiers left their barracks quietly and marched to the water front.

"Patriot spies followed them. They saw their fleet of small boats and barges in the moonlight. They found out where they were going. They were bound for Concord, twenty miles away, to seize the hidden patriot ammunition and guns the British spies had discovered.

"British spies had also discovered the hiding place in Lexington of our two great patriot leaders, Mr. John Hancock and Mr. Samuel Adams.

"The king had ordered their arrest because they had spoken so many times against the high taxes. His Majesty wanted them sent to England where they would be tried and hanged.

"Patriot spies had learned this only tonight. Certain English officers had talked too much.

"Now there was a Committee of Patriots in Boston. It was made up of leading citizens; important and wise men.

"The patriot spies reported to them at all times. You may be sure then they knew about the British troops in a few minutes. They had feared this would happen and they had been getting ready for it.

"They had managed to get guns and powder secretly. And patriot troops had been drilling secretly all the way from Boston to Concord.

"These troops must be warned that the British soldiers were coming. They must be told to hold them back long enough so the powder and guns

180

could be carted away from Concord to a new hiding place.

"But more important than that was the safety of Mr. Hancock and Mr. Adams. They must be warned to flee from Lexington immediately.

"A messenger must be sent at once. It would be a dangerous ride. Enemy scouts would be out to keep the roads clear for their troops.

"It would take a man of great courage. He must have good judgment. He must be able to think and act quickly if suddenly surrounded by the enemy.

"Above all, he must be a devoted patriot. He must be willing to lose his own life to save these great patriot leaders.

"There was one man they knew they could depend on. He was Mr. Paul Revere, the silversmith. He was forty years old now but he was strong and a splendid horseman.

"He was a devoted patriot, and he was one of

their spies. He had intelligence and he was trustworthy.

"But he had a wife and children. He had a fine business. Would he give all this up? Would he be willing to risk his life?

" 'Let Mr. Revere answer those questions himself,' said the president of the Committee. 'We will send for him.'

"In a few minutes Paul Revere came.

"Then they told him everything. They said the messenger must take the shortest route to Concord, for that was the direction in which the enemy troops were going.

"This messenger must cross the Charles River in a skiff. A horse would be waiting on the other side. Certain patriots were watching there now for a signal.

"Lights were to be shown in the belfry tower of the Old North Church. One light if the troops went by land. Two lights if they left by water.

" 'British spies would prevent this if they knew,' warned the Committee. 'You must be most careful at the church.'

"Also there was a British warship in the mouth of the river where he would have to cross. English marines would be patrolling her deck and it was a bright moonlight night. He might be captured then and put in chains on the man-of-war.

"Or he might be captured later, on the road. He might even lose his life.

"The danger was great from the moment he started his ride.

" 'We do not compel you to go,' said the Committee. 'We do not say it is your duty as a patriot. It is for you to decide.'

"Paul Revere didn't hesitate.

" 'I will go, gentlemen,' he said.

"One hundred years have passed but those words still ring in our hearts.

" 'I will go, gentlemen.' "

The speaker sat down. The bells now rang solemnly as if they knew the dangers ahead.

THE RIDE

The bells stopped. The second speaker stood on the platform and began:

"There was no time to lose. The messenger must cross the river before the troops crossed.

"Mr. Revere rushed home for a coat. Perhaps he wanted more to tell his family good-by.

"His last act that night took courage. He came here to the sexton's home where enemy soldiers were sleeping. He wakened the sexton and asked him to show two lighted lanterns in the belfry tower.

"This, he said, would be the signal to certain patriots across the river. It would tell them that British troops were leaving by water.

184

"The sexton promised to do this and went at once to get the lanterns. That is the reason we say the ride began here. We are proud to claim as one of us the sexton who hung those signal lights. He was a good patriot, also, this Mr. Robert Newman.

"And all this happened right under the noses of the sleeping soldiers upstairs.

"A little later Paul Revere was under the noses of the British cannon in the river.

"He had muffled his oars but they must have seen him from the man-of-war. However, they probably thought he was one of their own men crossing under orders from their General Gage.

"Anyway he was not stopped.

"These 'certain patriots' on the other shore had seen the signal. They had a horse saddled and waiting.

"Paul Revere mounted and galloped away on the road to Concord.

186

"He stopped at every farmhouse, village, and town. He pounded on doors.

" 'The British troops are coming!' he cried. 'Wake up! The enemy is upon you!'

"His words set church bells ringing all along the way. And the patriot troops in Lexington came running with their guns.

"They were rightly named, these minutemen. They came the minute they were called.

"Mr. Revere woke the two leaders in Lexington and told them to flee for their lives.

"And thanks to him, Mr. John Hancock and Mr. Samuel Adams were able to get to a place of safety.

"Thanks also to Paul Revere the outnumbered minutemen in Lexington held the British troops back long enough for the ammunition to be carted to a new hiding place.

"Thanks again to Paul Revere, the minutemen drove the enemy back to Boston.

"No wonder this midnight ride has become a part of American history. It gave Americans the chance to show the world they were determined to be free.

"They were determined no king or foreign country could give them orders and arrest their citizens.

"American freedom itself was on the move with Paul Revere that night."

AT THE REVERE HOUSE

The celebration continued that afternoon. It seemed that all of Boston was trying to get into the street in front of the "Revere House."

This was Paul Revere's home after he was married and during the Revolution.

His silversmith shop was here, too, in a large front room on the first floor.

The people talked about messages he carried

for the Committee of Patriots to other cities. They told about his long trips to New York City and Philadelphia where he was constantly in danger.

They said he carried secret messages to patriots in enemy country, surrounded by many enemy spies and enemy soldiers.

Yet he always returned safe and sound, so smart was he in the way he managed things.

Boston people were proud of him and church bells rang to welcome him home from these trips.

There was a great deal of talk about that night when he helped to throw English tea into the harbor—three hundred chests of it.

They said this was done to show the king that Boston patriots would not pay the new tea tax. They destroyed the tea so it couldn't be sold.

Paul Revere and his friends were disguised as Indians when they boarded the king's tea ships. But even then it was a daring act.

If they were found out they would be arrested and put in jail .

"The governor did try to find out who they were," said a man, "but no one seemed to know."

"Why, every patriot in Boston knew who they were," said a lady. "They knew that Paul Revere was the ringleader, too, but the secret was kept for years."

"Good! Good!" exclaimed some who had never heard this.

The bells of Christ Church now rang merrily and a man came from the "Revere House." He was a handsome man about forty years old. He looked very much like Paul Revere at that age. And he was dressed in the same kind of clothing Paul wore in his shop.

The people were so pleased with his appearance they clapped their hands.

The bells stopped ringing. The man said he would recite some verses Paul Revere wrote.

There were rhymes about the British generals.
The king got a good scoring, too.

The people laughed and clapped so long the
man had to raise his hand for silence. He said
he would now recite Henry W. Longfellow's
poem about the midnight ride of Paul Revere.

"Listen, my children, and you shall hear
Of the midnight ride of Paul Revere,
On the eighteenth of April, in seventy-five;
Hardly a man is now alive
Who remembers that famous day and year.

He said to his friend, "If the British march
By land or sea from the town to-night,
Hang a lantern aloft in the belfry arch
Of the North Church tower as a signal light,—

One, if by land, and two, if by sea;
And I on the opposite shore will be,
Ready to ride and spread the alarm
Through every Middlesex village and farm,
For the country folk to be up and to arm."

There were tears in many eyes as he finished
with this stanza:

"A hurry of hoofs in a village street,
A shape in the moonlight, a bulk in the dark,
And beneath, from the pebbles, in passing, a
    spark
Struck out by a steed flying fearless and fleet:
That was all! And yet, through the gloom and
    the light,
The fate of a nation was riding that night."